Exchange Rate

David Reynolds-Moreton

sci-fi-cafe.com

sci-fi-cafe.com

One:
The Return

THE FIRST THING he became aware of was a series of powerful vibrations that shook his body into wakefulness, and after several failed attempts he managed to force his reluctant eyes to open. Dim light filtered down through the blue green ice of the cavern's roof, reinforced by brilliant flashes as strike after strike of lightning bit into the solid mantle above.

The thunderous cacophony which accompanied every strike echoed around the cave, sending wave upon wave of piercing sound into his tortured eardrums.

Small shards of ice fell from above and showered him in a hail of stinging particles, while the pulses of raw energy raining down from the tortured sky built up an electrical charge in the surrounding ice which made every hair on his body stand on end.

He didn't know who, or where he was, and yet the echoing cavern seemed strangely familiar somehow. Desperately he tried to reach back into his memory to find the answers and was greeted with a vicious stab of pain which sent him reeling.

After the agonizing pulse had passed and his vision cleared, he tried to make some sense of his surroundings. He was in a huge circular ice cave which didn't look as if it had occurred naturally as it was so symmetrical, while the ice crystals behind the smooth gleaming surface refracted the flashes of lightning from above into a myriad of scintillating stars.

The only exit from the glass-like cavern was a passageway to his left, also perfectly cut into the ice.

What the hell am I doing here? brought no answer, so he tried to recall where he had been before awakening and finding himself entombed in the ice cave.

He reeled, as again the flash of pain seared through his head leaving him feeling sick and dizzy for his trouble.

Slowly he began to realise that looking around the cave caused no problems, but looking back into his memory for answers that lay in the past triggered the pain pulse. For the time being at least, he decided to keep his thoughts strictly in the present and leave the past alone until he could figure out what was happening to him.

The pain had gone, and the dizzy feeling was slowly fading away as he again tried to take stock of his surroundings. The cave seemed the right place to be in, almost as though he had been there before, and yet he had the feeling that he had only just arrived.

The lightning strikes were lessening by the minute, and with them the pulses of vivid fire that flickered around the walls of the cavern.

With one last half-hearted rumble the electric storm moved away, and his eyes grew more accustomed to the soft and gentle pale green light which filtered down through the ice high above him.

Looking down on himself, he was surprised to see a massive body supported by four sturdy well muscled legs terminating in large padded feet, each equipped with six huge claws.

The underside of his feet were covered with course bristle like hair which gripped the ice very effectively, while the claws moved slickly in and out of their sheaths like pieces of well oiled machinery.

His trunk curved upwards from the forelegs into a broad chest atop of which was a thick neck supporting a head.

Near the top of his chest were a pair of arms equally as well built as his legs, and equipped with five digits in one plane and an opposing digit. Thumb seemed to be the right name somehow,

But why ... stop! He wasn't going to invite the pain pulse again if he could help it.

'That's odd' he thought, finding a tail on the rear end of his body. 'But why was it odd?...' It started off as thick as his arm and tapered off to a fine point some three metres from the base.

His body was covered in a thick silver white hair which glistened in the pale light of the cave, and seeing a somewhat distorted reflection of himself in the ice wall, he could not help thinking what a fine looking creature stood before him.

Raising his head to its full extent, he opened his mouth and emitted a roar that thundered around the ice cavern, shaking a few loose fragments of cracked ice from the vaulted dome above him. Although he didn't know what to expect, he didn't anticipate the tremendous blast of sound which had occurred.

He was more startled than surprised, and flicked his tail to and fro, finally bringing it down on the ice with a thwack that reverberated around the cavern like a pistol shot.

Sitting back on his haunches and curling his tail protectively around his legs, he again tried to take stock of the strange situation he found himself in. Although it made little sense, he felt the cave was his base or home, whatever that was, and he belonged here.

He was aware of being himself, but not necessarily the body which he seemed to be in, and that seemed a bit bizarre as well. But thinking about it, he must be the creature with the silver white hair, as it moved and did his bidding without pause for thought, and yet he was aware of being himself, separately somehow.

Maybe the terrific static charge which had built up in the cavern due to the electric storm had messed up his thinking processes somewhat, but that explanation didn't seem any more real than the rest of the situation he found himself in, and he rejected it for the time being.

It was no good, he would have to sort that one out when he had found a way to get around the pain pulses every time he tried to think back into the past, as he felt sure that somewhere deep in his memory was where the answers to his present predicament lay.

Glancing around the cavern again he saw a large metal box over by the wall, and getting to his feet, he staggered a little as he went over to investigate it.

There seemed to be a top to it which lifted up, and peering inside he saw a collection of deep purple crystals. All of a sudden, memory flood back in.

He was supposed to collect the crystals and place them in the box, and when it was full....he was not sure, but got the idea that it was to be exchanged for something he needed, but he didn't really need anything, as far as he knew.

He had food, a little pile of it was near the box, a collection of pale yellow pod-like things which grew in the softer parts of the ice field outside the cavern. What else did he need?

Suddenly the pain was back, not at full strength, but enough to hurt, and then he remembered.

He was supposed to put a crystal in the box, and a clear pale amber capsule of some sort was dispensed from a slot at the bottom.

The capsule when taken made the pain go away for a while, and then he had to go outside to look for another crystal, hoping to find one before the pain came back and grew too bad to withstand.

The pain had eased a little, but was still there in the background, reminding him of the task ahead. A flash of anger swept through him as he realised that someone or something had him trapped in a vicious circle, and he had no option other than to collect the crystals or suffer, and he resented it deeply.

Shaking off the shower of scintillating ice crystals he had acquired when first giving voice in the ice cavern, he slowly made his way to the tunnel exit, while stiff muscles complained bitterly at having to move his huge bulk before warming up.

Moving down through the passageway, little bits of memory came back in the form of pictures. He knew somehow where to look for the crystals, and that they were needed very badly by someone or something, but who or why was beyond him for the moment.

Knowing somehow that he would be rewarded if he could find enough of them, he then remembered that the box had to be placed on a large flat black rock outside the cave.

Something would come down out of the sky and take the box, returning it later for him to fill again.

At the tunnel exit he had a restricted view of the surrounding terrain, as a curtain of mist hung like a dirty grey veil obscuring his vision of the horizon.

The ice field stretched off into the distance for a few hundred metres and then disappeared as a swirling blizzard of ice crystals swept around him, reducing his vision even further to a couple of metres for a while.

The wind moaned and groaned as it funnelled it's way through the jagged outcrops of blue ice to his left, and then swept up over the huge ice cliff in which his home had been constructed. Odd that he thought of it as home, as he had no extant memory of being there before now.

As the swirling ice cloud lessened a little, he could just make out to his right the black platform of the rock on which the box of crystals had to be placed for collection, and which would then hopefully be returned empty of crystals, but containing the pain relieving capsules which he instinctively knew he was going to need in the future.

The wind had died down to some extent, and with it the swirling clouds of stinging ice crystals. Now that he could see a little further, he remembered that the last lot of crystals had been found some two kilometres past the black rock and a little to the right of the track which he had worn in the ice sheet on previous trips. Previous trips...? No, leave that thought for now.

As the pain was still nagging away at the back of his head, he resolved to go down the track to the place where he had found crystals before, and see if there were any more. He progressed slowly down the sloping track, realising the necessity for those massive sharp claws, for without them he would not be able to stand upright for very long as the wind coming up the incline was gusting at about one hundred kilometres an hour, and with a steady component of at least eighty.

The razor sharp claws bit into the rock hard ice as if it were soft ground, relinquishing their grip automatically as each foot was lifted for the next step.

He didn't have to think about it at all, it just happened as he walked carefully along the trail, which by now, was a little fainter than before as the old claw marks were being filled in with chips of airborne ice, the particles being fused into the track by the sheer velocity of the driving wind.

The ice crystals stung his eyes a little, but the thick membrane that covered them took most of the force out of the torrent of particles and so didn't cause him too much discomfort, as long as he didn't face directly into the blast.

What was left of the old track curved away from the patch of softice where he had previously found some of the yellow pods which formed his diet. As more had grown since his last hazily remembered visit, he decided to collect them on the way back to the cavern

Last visit? He didn't remember being here before, and yet the same strange feeling, almost dreamlike, that he knew this place well, too well in fact, and anger began to swell up inside him again, followed by a short burst of pain to tell him to stay off that subject for now.

The pathway abruptly came to an end with a sheer drop of some three metres or so, the ice plate having split away from the main body of ice and dropped to a new level. He stopped short in his tracks.

This usually meant that a large movement of the ice plate was about to take place, and here was perhaps not a good place to be when it happened.

If he went back now and waited for the ice to settle down the increasing pain would be too much to allow him to sleep, so he must press on come what may, and recover another crystal and so get his pain relieving capsule.

Judging the distance carefully, he jumped down to the next level, landing in a shower of blue green chips of ice and slithering some six metres before coming to a halt.

This was dangerous, as the ice sheet must be extra soft for him to have slipped so far, and if it had been a narrow ledge he had landed on, it could have meant a serious fall.

Was he getting careless or were the conditions on this planet undergoing change? As he looked back to the level above, there was the squeal of ice being twisted almost to breaking point, followed by a deafening crack and the surface beneath him heaved and sank another two metres with a massive shudder.

He carefully studied the shear five metre wall of clear ice that now lay before him, and realised that to get back up to the level above was going to be difficult, if not impossible.

Perhaps there was another way up a little further along the rift, where the ice had not fallen quite so far.

He decided to collect the crystals first, if any were in the vicinity, and then worry about reaching the main ice sheet above.

The track made by his previous visits was all but obliterated by the driving ice particles, and he had to go on what he felt was the right direction, looking for an outcrop of the red crumbling rock which was the main source of the purple crystals.

The outcrops didn't always contain crystals, or if they did, they were beyond his reach without tools to cut into the harder core of the stone. Usually he managed to find at least one crystal in every three rocks searched, so the odds were to some extent in his favour.

The breakup of the ice sheet had proved to be more of a help than a hindrance, in as much that a large section of the main plate had slid sideways, revealing the rock layer beneath and thereby increasing his chances of finding the necessary crystal bearing substrate.

He estimated the drop down to solid ground was only a couple of metres, and he could easily jump back up again from that height, as long as nothing else moved in the mean time.

Looking over the edge of the ice, he checked to make sure that the ground really was solid, and not like the softice which sometimes gave way under his weight, and had nearly drowned him once. It looked firm enough to take his weight, so he chanced it.

He jumped down to the stony layer below and looked around to make sure all was well, and that the ground was as solid as it looked. The exposed surface of the planet was hard and uneven compared to the ice he usually travelled over, and his claws could not get such a good grip on it as the points would not penetrate the hard crystalline surface.

Moving slowly and warily so as not to be caught by a sudden movement of the ice above, he made his way along the rift, looking for the telltale signs of the red outcrop that would herald the possibility of a crystal, and so bring some relief from the pain which was by now demanding his attention to the exclusion of all else, and that was a dangerous position to be in.

So far, there had been no red outcrops, and with mounting

impatience he increased his speed towards the end of the rift.

An ear splitting screech rent the air, as once again the stresses built up in the ice, and it twisted to breaking point.

There was a sullen silence, even the ever present wind seemed frozen for a moment in time, and then there was an almighty crackling sound followed by a giant pistol shot as several thousand tonnes of ice parted company from the main sheet above, and crashed down all around him.

Despite his huge weight, reflex action sponsored a powerful leap backwards which found him safely on the unbroken ice surface behind, with only a few bruises instead of broken limbs.

As the frozen blocks settled in their new positions, he saw a large slab of the red rock he had been seeking protruding from the new ice face, and warily he made his way down to the ground below. Being careful no to be caught out again by the ever moving ice sheet, he approached the rock slowly, listening for the faintest sign of creaking from the frozen terrain above him.

Slowly the giant claws removed layer upon layer of the soft crumbling outer skin of the rock, applying more and more pressure as the rocky substrate itself grew harder as he worked towards the core, and then he found the crystal. It was the biggest one he had ever seen, nearly a metre in length and with a girth to match.

Gently he eased it from its birthplace in the rocky mass and marvelled at its crystalline beauty.

It was much like the other crystals he had collected, except this one was of an unusual clarity and size, and the deepest purple he had ever seen, almost black.

Surely this specimen is worth at least two capsules, he thought, knowing full well that the box only released one capsule per crystal, irrespective of size or quality.

He wondered what would happen if he could drive something into the cavity from which the crystal had come, so splitting the rock open.

After a lengthy search, he found a wedge shaped splinter of stone that would just about enter the cavity, and he rammed it in as far as it would go.

Picking up another stone, he used it as a hammer to drive the wedge into the main rock as far as he could. Almost soundlessly the red rock split open to reveal two more crystals, not of the same size as the first one, but worth collecting just the same.

This was the first time he had found more than one crystal in the same piece of rock, and wondered how many more he had missed in the past through ignorance and not looking any further than the soft surface layer of the crystal bearing substrate. Feeling very pleased with his discovery, he wondered how best to maximise the benefits of the extra two crystals.

As far as he could remember, the crystal gathering was a daily chore and somewhat resented. Now, with three crystals, he could take a couple of days off from his usual routine... but to do what? Sit around the ice cave? Go exploring? But I do that anyway, when looking for crystals, he thought. What else could he do with the time he had potentially gained from the bonus crystals?

Nothing really, which he didn't normally do. Feeling somewhat disappointed, he checked the remains of the red rock lumps for any missed crystals and then looked around for an easy way out of the rift.

There was another squeal from the ice, and a large slab broke off from the main sheet with a loud crack and crashed in fragments at his feet. Something was making the ice move more than usual, and this worried him. Going over to the new fracture, he notice that the ground was noticeably warm compared to the ice surrounding it, and this was something new.

He knew that softice was not as cold as the main ice sheets, but this new warmth in the underlying rock was totally unexpected. Somewhere in the back of his mind a cord was struck, a faint memory of something to do with plate tectonics and vulca... no, it was gone, but he knew he did have the answers to the warm rocks if only he could delve back far enough into his memory.

The pain was getting steadily worse, and he looked forward to the time when he could drop the crystal into the box and get his pain relieving capsule.

The newly broken ice turned to slush beneath his feet before he reached the tumbled blocks up which he then scrambled to the firm ice sheet above. It was not unlike softice, but no food plants grew in it as far as he could tell.

There's a thought, maybe the softice had warm rocks beneath it, but as there was nowhere for the slush to go it just lay there and the plants grew in it to produce the yellow pods. He found the track he had made on his outward journey, and turned for home with a good feeling about the day's discoveries.

There was no more heaving of the ground as he wended his way back to the ice cavern, so he though about the food pods.

They grew in softice, and that was caused by warm ground beneath the ice field. But where did the pods come from in the first place? The idea of seeds came to mind, and then a whole block of memory fell into place.

Of course, the seeds were in the ground waiting for a temperature rise so that they could germinate. So perhaps there maybe more plants which would grow if the temperature was high enough. It might just be possible that this world was not as cold as it is now, and plants flourished all over the place. His thoughts raced on and on, spurred along with each regained piece of memory.

Without realising it, he had arrived back at the entrance to the ice cavern, and was about to go in when he noticed another storm front on the horizon.

These damn storms are getting more frequent than is comfortable, he thought, as he made his way into the tunnel. He didn't usually venture out during a really bad storm as the wind was sufficient to cause him to lose his footing, and once over he would be at the mercy of the hurricane force blast and blinded by the driving ice particles.

Hurrying over to the metal box he lifted the lid and dropped the smaller of the three crystals in, closing the lid carefully so as to give the mechanism the necessary signal to release his anti-pain capsule.

Once he had been in such a hurry to acquire the pain relieving drug that he had inadvertently dropped the lid down with a bang, and no capsule was dispensed. By the time he had found another crystal, the pain level was causing his vision to blur and waves of retching on an already empty stomach were adding to the agony.

That had been a lesson he wouldn't forget in a hurry, and was certainly not going to risk the experience again. He needed all his awareness to survive in this hostile place.

Waiting for the mechanism to release the pain killer, he noticed that the casing was showing signs of corrosion and hoped it would soon be considered full enough with the crystals to warrant placing on the black 'launch pad' outside, when it would go up into the sky and return with another supply of the much needed capsules.

His memory was returning in ever increasing amounts as he pieced together the little bits of data he had gathered from the environment and from previous recollections.

The box was only ready for exchange when the slot at the bottom had snapped shut after the last capsule had been dispensed, and then, and only then, would the black rock send the signal for the retrieval of the box and its subsequent return.

So the black rock was not of this world, he reasoned, and must be part of the system that held him prisoner here, causing him to suffer if he didn't do their bidding. Anger welled up again as he realised he had no control over his destiny, and was powerless to change it. Or was he? Somewhere hidden in his memory there was a feeling that something could be done, but he couldn't recall just what it was at the moment.

A faint click heralded the arrival of the precious capsule as the release mechanism went into action, and the pain relieving drug rolled out onto the ice. Picking up the tiny object was always a problem as his fingers were so big compared to that which had to be retrieved, and placing it in his mouth was not much easer.

There was a faint tingling as the capsule dissolved in the warmth of his mouth and released it's cargo of pain killing chemicals, and a few seconds later the ache in his head began to subside. He lay back on the ice floor, grinning to himself as he cradled the two remaining crystals in his hands.

Somehow he felt the system was not unbeatable, and he should be able to find a way of getting out of this never ending treadmill of an existence.

The recurring thought that someone or something else had total control over him and what he did, brought another flush of anger, spoiling the good feeling he had experienced having gained the two extra crystals. How best to use to use the extra crystals? He pondered this for a while, looking at all possible ways in which they could be used to beat the system and provide some gain for him.

Perhaps he could get two capsules out of the box, using one as required to ease the pain, and save the other for a time when he had difficulty in finding a crystal.

And then he vaguely remembered having tried that before, but the clear capsule had gone cloudy after a few moments and then dissolved into a foul smelling mush.

Maybe there was a way in which he could preserve the capsules for future use, but he hadn't found it yet. He realised he would have to simulate the conditions of the box from which they came, but how?

By now the distant rumblings of the approaching weather front had grown into the customary flash, crash and bang of a fully fledged storm. The blue and purple lightning strikes lit up the cavern through the thick ice roof, the high energy bolts of electrical discharge ripping the very molecules of the atmosphere asunder, and no doubt, forming new combinations of chemicals in the process.

For some reason the storms seemed to be getting ever more violent in nature, and he certainly wouldn't even consider being caught out in one now as he had done in the past. Was this part of the planet undergoing some sort of major change? Life was difficult enough without having to endure the restriction imposed by the vicious ice storms.

The temperature of the ground in certain areas was higher than he could recall, and the increasing frequency and violence of the storms indicated that a major change of some sort was under way. He dreaded to think just what effect it would have on him and the task he was forced to perform.

The storm roared and crashed above the cavern, sending the odd shower of splintered ice crystals down from above, while the lightning lit up the walls in a cascade of flickering star like fires, the ice refracting the light into a multitude of spangled colours.

He didn't mind the storm any more, as the pain in his head had gone and he was safe in his cavern. Mulling over the events of his crystal hunting expedition, his revere was suddenly shattered as the wind velocity increased to a deafening howl, and the pressure wave thundered into the tunnel causing his ears to pop.

This had never happened before, as far as he could remember, and a little runnel of fear ran through him. Would successive pressure waves be sufficient to blow the cavern roof out and expose him to the fall fury of the storm?

He moved over to the wall of the cave as this seemed to be the safest place to be while the electric storm vented it's fury on the world outside.

The extra crystals were forgotten, surviving the storm was upper most in his mind. He felt naked fear for the first time that he could recall, and he felt a strange excitement.

His huge form was tensed up in a huddle, tight against the cavern wall when a massive lightning strike ripped through the cavern roof, filling the space below with a shower of ice particles and a static charge that caused a spasmodic twitch in every muscle of his body. There was no where to run.

Outside the raging storm would toss him about like a food pod or bury him under an avalanche of shattered ice.

All he could do was wait the storm out, and hope for the best. He would dearly have liked to get his hands on those responsible for his present predicament, and make them change places with him.

How long the storm had torn into the ice above he had no idea, but at long last the crash and rumble seemed to be receding into the distance.

The gaping hole in the roof of the cavern let in the odd blast of subzero air with it's accompanying flurry of ice crystals, and he wondered if it would be possible to repair the hole by dropping ice blocks into it from the outside before the cavern filled up, and he would have no refuge from subsequent storms.

With an air of resignation to the inevitable, he shook the encrusted ice from his coat and made his way slowly down the tunnel to the outside world.

The exit of the passageway was partially blocked with huge chunks of ice from the shattered pinnacles that had been his landmark for the cavern entrance, together with drift ice which the storm had swept along as it channelled its way up from the lower ice plain and over the ledge below the cliff.

It was now going to be more difficult to find the cave again if he lost sight of the tracks he made when he went out searching for crystals, as they could so easily be filled with ice crystals if the wind was strong enough.

Somehow the storm must have scooped up a few of the larger blocks of free ice and sent them crashing into the tower-like buttresses that stood by the tunnel opening, smashing them into the rubble of ice which he now had to claw his way through. Hurriedly he ripped away at the blockage, as if left for too long it would fuse into a solid lump and would then be impossible to move.

From past experience he knew that freshly piled up ice blocks, due to their weight pressing on one another, caused a melting at the points where they touched, and when the melt water had run off, the blocks would refreeze into one amorphous block.

Having broken his way out of the tunnel and cleared away the debris, he took stock of the new scene. Gone were the old familiar landmarks he knew so well, along with the ice ledge that had led into his cave. It had been ripped away by the abrasive effect of loose ice as it was propelled along at a horrendous speed by the storm winds.

He had never seen such violent changes in the landscape from just one storm, things which had been difficult but predictable were beginning to change on the planet, and he was reacquainted with the fear of uncertainty once again.

The hole in the cave roof was his first priority, and that had to be sealed from the action of future storms.

Climbing up the ice cliff was made a little easier as the pack ice had been plastered to the cliff walls and gave a good foot hold.

Driving his talons into the newly formed blocks, he gradually made his way to the top of the cliff for the first time, and was surprised by what he saw.

Stretching away to the distant horizon was the newly polished main ice sheet, stripped of all its lumps and bumps and now completely featureless, except for one lone ice column. Over to his right the ice cliff continued in an unbroken line, until it met and merged with the giant ice mountain chain that had formed a barrier to his previous explorations.

Many times he had wanted to explore the Ice Mountains and see what lay beyond them, but they had always appeared impassable.

Turning around he could now see the area below on the lower ice sheet where he had previously hunted for the crystals and food pods. Large areas of loose ice had been blown away by the storm, exposing the stony ground beneath. This would make his hunting that little bit easier in the future if the next storm didn't cover it all up again.

His attention now turned to the business in hand, the blocking up of the hole in the roof of the ice cavern. The one remaining ice column looked lone and stark on the otherwise barren ice sheet, and in a strange way he felt loathe to destroy it, but he needed to fill the hole in his roof.

He soon covered the fifty metres to the column, and was relieved to see that the scurrying ice had whittled away the base, leaving him only a small amount of ice to cut away to bring the whole thing down.

His claws slashed at the base of the column, sending showers of scintillating ice crystals into the air, and not a few in his eyes. There was a loud crack, and he jumped back as the huge column of ice came crashing down, luckily not breaking into useless fragments.

Putting his shoulder to the now recumbent ice block, he slowly and carefully edged it down the gentle slope towards the lip of the ice sheet, looking for the hole in the roof of the cave. As it neared the edge, the block picked up speed on the now increasing slope, and all he could do was guide it with a sideways push as the sheer mass of the ice was too much for him to stop.

The Gods, if Gods there be, were on his side, as the huge block of ice upended itself and slid into the waiting hole with a satisfying crunch, he only just managed to dig his claws into the ice to stop himself going over the edge of the ice sheet to a drop of some one hundred and fifty metres.

Next he had to get back to the cavern, and was reluctant to try and climb down the ice blocks he had ascended as doing so would be more dangerous than the climb up. Perhaps there was another way down a little further along, and so he set off along the edge, looking for a return route a little less hazardous than the journey up.

The hardness and glass-like quality of the ice sheet surprised him, glass? What was glass?, and then it came back to him. A clear transparent sheet of something, windows, buildings. The pictures were coming thick and fast and his head reeled under the impact of so much recall.

Some pictures seemed familiar while others made no sense at all, and when he tried to look deeper he received a sharp stab of pain for his troubles, and the general pain in his head was getting worse, so he knew he must return soon to get the pain reliving capsule, he also felt the first pangs of hunger coming on.

After a kilometre or so, he saw a steep slope down to the lower levels. It was a long way down, but if he went down backwards and used his claws as a braking mechanism, there was a chance he could make it without too much damage. As the pain in his head increased, his mind was made up for him as he approached the edge of the ice sheet.

Lowering his rear end over the lip of the main ice sheet he let go, and was soon speeding down to the lower level a lot faster than he was comfortable with. The huge claws dug in deeply, sending a shower of ice crystals high into the air with a hideous screech and his velocity decreased a little, but he still wound up in an undignified heap at the bottom of the slope.

Looking around he saw thin wisps of mist forming in the distance, and realised that if it grew any thicker he would have difficulty in finding his cavern.

The towering blue-green ice cliffs to his left gave an indication of just how high he had been when on the main ice sheet above, and explained the speed of his somewhat ungraceful descent to this level. And then he saw the hole in the ice wall, not unlike the entrance to his own cave.

Curiosity got the better of him, and he approached the opening cautiously. Light filtering from above gave the place an eerie glow which was different to the light he was used to in his own cavern. The ice beneath his feet turned to slush, and then muddy stones and flat rock. The odd rock jutted out from the ice walls every now and then, indicating that the ice had moved and picked up the rocks in its travel.

The passageway grew darker as he went in, the ice now giving way to solid rock and the light changed from pale green to a yellow hue. He was not expecting there to be any light at all this far in, and it seemed to be getting brighter as he progressed.

The rocky walls were covered in what seemed to be a fine mossy growth which gave out the gentle yellow light, and when he touched it with his fingers, they too glowed with their own weird light.

He was now torn between going on to see what lay ahead and the nagging pain in his head. The pain was insidiously increasing, so he decided to return to his cavern and come back some other time when he was free of the call to the capsule box.

There was just about enough room for him to turn around, and he then made his way back to the outside world and the search for home.

He had only gone a few metres, when the ice gave way with a sharp crack and he found himself up to his shoulders in softice. It took all his not inconsiderable strength to haul himself out of the slush pool.

He shook his mighty body to rid himself of the considerable quantity of soft clinging ice he had acquired, lest it froze on him and he became just another weird shape in an even more weird world.

A rift in the ice sheet just ahead revealed an area of stony ground which had been cleared of ice blocks by the violent winds of the storm, and there lay several lumps of the red rock which usually held the much sort after crystals. The first rock just crumbled away to reveal nothing, but the next one yielded two crystals of the deepest purple.

By the time he had checked all the rocks and reduced them to piles of red rubble, he had acquired nine crystals, much to his amazement. The hungry collecting box could now be fed for some time without much effort on his part, and that would give him plenty of time to explore the newly found tunnel in the ice cliff.

He realised that some means of carrying a large number of items such as the crystals and food pods required a bag made of some sort of material. The very thought of a 'material' brought a sharp stab of pain to be added to the already nagging ache in his head, so he dropped the idea for the time being.

The cavern entrance was a welcoming sight, and he hurried up the tunnel to the inner chamber.

The ice block had done its job of sealing the hole in the roof, with just a metre showing through, but well above head height.

Hastily he put the crystals down with the others and selecting the smallest one, approached the collecting box, lifted the lid, and gently placed the crystal on the ledge within. What seemed like an age passed before the box verified it was indeed a crystal, and almost reluctantly emitted its customary click, dispensing the capsule from the slot at its base.

He went though the usual fumbling routine of picking up the capsule and placed it in his mouth. Within seconds it had melted and its contents began to ease the pain which had by now almost reached eye watering proportions.

These crystals must mean an awful lot to someone, he mused, Because of the complexity of the system set up to get them. He couldn't understand why they didn't come themselves. There must be a very good reason why not, he thought, as he relaxed to let the rest of the pain ebb away.

There were only three food pods left and he began to worry in case the storm had swept away all the softice, and they only grew in that medium.

His stomach was urgently requesting food, so he threw caution to the wind, and ate all three pods, hoping more could be found without too much trouble.

Still thinking about the events of the last few hours, he drifted into a fitful sleep, and dreamt about strange little two legged creatures which stood upright and waved their arms about at him.

He couldn't understand why they didn't fall over as they moved about. And they used strange words, some of which seemed familiar while others meant nothing at all. And then there was this tunnel with the strange yellow light....

The planet continued to transfer its orbit from one twin sun to the other, causing the climate change he had witnessed, but did not understand.

Due to the core of the planet being off centre, which in it self was an extreme rarity, it always had the same surface facing one of the planets, and at switch over it took some time for the whole system to re-stabilise, hence the rapid melting of he ice sheet, the storm winds and a general shake up of stresses which had built up over time since the last change over.

One side of the planet was under the constant blast of light and heat from whichever sun it orbited around at the time, while the other was permanently shrouded in thick ice many kilometres thick.

Around the equator was a temperate zone with ice on one side and an area of hot rock on the other, a mountain range shielded the temperate zone from excessive heat, allowing life to flourish in all its varied forms.

Nature, for want of a better word, will always fill every tiny gap which is remotely habitable, and some of its creations take on the most bizarre forms in order to fit into what most would consider a totally hostile environment.

The twin sun system with it's lone planet was a rare freak of nature which brought about some of the more unusual minerals to be found there, Violent electric storms, caused by the massive clouds of ice crystals being shunted about from one side of the planet to the other, added their immense power to the formation of these new minerals, some of which had never been found anywhere else in the known universe.

The atmosphere was also a casualty of this strange arrangement, being corrosive in the extreme to anything alien to the parent planet.

He woke up with a start. A loud crash of falling ice echoed up through tunnel. He slowly stretched his body out to its fullest length, arching his back until the vertebra clicked.

Feeling fully rested, and in a much more reasonable state of mind, he went outside to see what had awakened him.

One of the few remaining buttresses had given way, and scattered its remains around the tunnel entrance.

Now that he was up and about, he realised he should go looking for food pods, lest some other catastrophe should remove what few there may be left.

The wind having died down, the atmosphere cleared again and he could see for some considerable distance now, almost out to the far horizon, although fine detail was still a little hazy.

Padding along at a comfortable jog, he was soon at the edge of the terrain that was known to him, and he now ventured out onto the unexplored expanse of ice that eventually lead up to the distant dark blue ice mountains.

A small area of softice lay to one side of the ledge he was on, so he diverted off his intended path to investigate it.

The patch was a little different than usual, as the centre of the area was stony ground, and a group of pod plants were in the middle of it. He had never seen pods growing on or in anything other than softice so he approached them with caution.

The slush gave way to firmer ground as he neared the cluster of pods and he noticed they were different to the usual ones he had found, insofar that flat brownish plates were attached to the base of the plants and 'leaves' came to mind, although it meant little to him at the moment.

Each pod was surrounded by its little group of brownish leaves, with small yellowish shoots sprouting out from the base of the plant. In the past all he had seen was just the pods sticking up out of the softice.

So the leaves could have been there all the time and I missed them as they lay buried.

Among the yellow pods he was used to gathering were a few with brown stripes on the normal yellow, and he wondered if these might be edible, so he picked a few to try.

One of the plants must have been the first to produce pods as it was much taller than the others and the little brown leaves around the base seemed withered while the pods had an old and dry look about them.

When he tried to pull one off the plant it split, and several small black seeds flew out onto the ground.

Seeds, that rang a bell in his memory, and as the pictures came flooding in he just relaxed, resisting the urge to look deeper. There was no pain in his head this time. And then he realised that as long as he didn't probe into his mind and just let the memory pictures run, he could acquire information from the past without the searing pain in his head.

Gathering up as many pods as he could carry, he set off for the cavern determined to beat the system which had been set up to lock him into this awful situation of pain, hunger and looking for the crystals, whether he wanted to or not.

He had gone only a few hundred metres when with no warning, a huge section of ice just in front of him disappeared into a hole in the ground with a deafening roar.

Cautiously he went to the edge of the hole and was horrified to see a chasm nearly fifty metres across, and seemingly bottomless. The sides were smooth and reminded him of something which hovered on the edge of his awareness for a moment, and then was gone.

How many holes like this exist under the ice? Was his first thought, and how could he avoid them? He couldn't think of any way to be forewarned, except to listen out for the slightest sound of ice breaking, but it was doing that all the time.

Having gained the old track he had come out on and feeling a little more secure, he hurried on to the now somewhat doubtful sanctuary of the ice cavern.

He stacked the supply of pods next to the collecting box, sat down with his back to the cavern wall and after satisfying his hunger, contemplated his situation.

Not only was he still in mystery about his presence here, but things didn't seem right about the environment either.

He felt he belonged here as some things seemed so familiar, and yet he had no extant memory of this world. He could understand the cycle of crystal gathering but not the enforcement of it with the head pains. And then there was the agonising pain stab if he tried to dig into his memory.

He concluded that someone didn't want him to remember what it was all about, and that made him even angrier.

With a good supply of food pods, which he thought could be preserved for some time if he buried them in ice, and enough crystals to feed the collecting box for a while, he thought he could have some free time, if only the anti pain capsules could be preserved. He would have to simulate the conditions of the collecting box in which they were stored, but what were those conditions?

He had a hazy recollection of getting two capsules out once, taking one and then watching the other one slowly turn to a stinking mush, so perhaps it was the atmosphere that destroyed them? Could they be preserved in ice he wondered? Maybe digging a hole in a block of ice, putting the capsule in and then blocking the hole with a plug of ice would preserve them? He would give it a try.

The other thing that worried him was the changes taking place in the world outside. He could not recall such mighty storms before, or the ice sheet breaking up and such large pools of softice. It helped him locate food pods more easily, and likewise the crystals, so maybe it was not all bad.

Having brought some ice in from the broken fragments which lay around outside the cavern, he set about covering the food pods, and then chose a suitable block of ice in which to make a hole for a capsule. Pressure from a claw soon produced the necessary hole, and a small crystal coaxed the box to disgorge a capsule. Getting it into the hole in the ice was another matter with his clumsy fingers.

After much fumbling and his frustration level reaching a new peak, the capsule was safely entombed in the ice block and an ice plug fitted. As there was no day or night as such, and thinking about that brought another flood of pictures to mind, he decided he would leave the capsule in the ice for one collecting cycle, and if it was still viable after that time, he would have gained a little more control over the system.

Feeling very pleased with himself, he tried to recall the first awakening in the ice cavern and then where he was before... a blast of pain sent his senses reeling. Wiping the tears from his eyes and now feeling very tired, he curled up to take a much needed sleep. Dreams came and went, most of which made little sense, but he did remember one when he awoke about the strange little creatures with two legs, and they seemed very angry about something, and he was involved somehow.

A dull ache reminded him it was time for another capsule, and after going through the crystal routine he ate some food pods with a generous helping of ice crystals and wondered what to do next. And then he recalled the tunnel he had seen returning from the upper ice sheet. He would explore that.

There was a strange calmness outside, the wind had dropped to a whisper and the sky seemed brighter than usual. Thin tendrils of mist hung about in the gullies of the lower ice sheet, writhing about like sad ghosts as the gentle breeze moved them from hollow to hollow.

Sticking to what he though was the thickest ice, he moved swiftly along under the huge ice cliff which divided his known world from that of the mysteries of the upper ice sheet. The cave entrance came into sight, a beckoning black hole in the otherwise pristine white of his world, and he cautiously entered it. Nothing much seemed to have changed as he entered the rocky tunnel.

At first it grew darker, and then in the distance he could see the faint soft yellow glow of the strange light giving moss which clung to the walls of the tunnel. The floor of the passage was flat, smooth, and seemingly dust free, and that didn't seem right somehow, and then he noticed a gentle drift of air coming in behind him, perhaps that swept the dust away, but it didn't seem strong enough.

The tunnel was now quite well lit, the moss-like substance thickly covering the walls, but not the floor, and that seemed odd too. He concluded he would have to get used to unusual things in this strange world, and not worry about them so much.

The deeper he went into the mountain range beneath the great ice sheet, the warmer it got, and although it was not too uncomfortable, his thick coat of hair was adding to the problem as it was intended for the ice cold world outside.

A hole in the tunnel wall revealed a cave-like structure, like half a giant bubble, the walls of which glowed with the ever present moss. Along with the normal yellow, there were several shades of green and even a pale blue. He stood staring in amazement for a while, and wondered what other wonders the underworld of the mountain held.

He left the cave, still marvelling at its beauty, when he noticed the tunnel took a downwards slope, turned to the left and then expanded to a much greater width. Another opening in the tunnel wall led to a cave of even more shocking content. Nearly twenty metres in diameter and perfectly circular, the walls were studded with hundreds of purple crystals. They seemed to shine with a light of their own, almost dazzling, and he had to half close his eyes to see the finer details of the cave.

He stood there, spellbound for....he didn't know, it seemed like an eternity, almost as if time had stopped and he was in the cave's own time stream.

He backed out of the cave, almost in a state of reverence and stood still in the tunnel for some time, trying to get a feeling of reality again.

A shudder rippled through his body, and he was back to normal. The 'hair' cave, when he came to it, made him feel very uneasy. The walls were festooned with two metre long strands of silver white hair, exactly like his own coat, and he then realised that was why he felt disturbed by it.

Without quite knowing why, he reached for a clump of hair and gave it a tug. The second tug made him jump as the hair came away in his hand, leaving a bare patch on the cave wall. 'This could be a useful material' he thought, and feeling a little guilty, pulled several more clumps of hair from the walls.

Returning to the tunnel, he placed the bundle of hair down on the floor, intending to pick it up on his return journey to the outside world.

A soft rushing sound now accompanied his footfalls as he went deeper into the mountain, and the draft he could feel on his back increased a little.

Some twenty metres on, an opening in the tunnel wall drew his attention. Looking in through a metre sized hole he could see long streamers of a green coloured growth glistening with wetness, while a stream of water cascaded down the centre of the shaft.

Suddenly something long and dark green slithered out from the foliage, stared at him with two pin point jet black eyes, and then disappeared from sight up the shaft.

This was the first sign of active life he had seen in this world, apart for his own reflection in a softice pool, and it left him feeling very disturbed. Extra care must now be taken in case he came across something larger which didn't like its domain invaded by him.

Walking as quietly as possible so as to be able to pick up any sounds made by anything else, he continued on down the tunnel, but now the light level was dropping and the walls were only covered in patches of light giving moss.

Soon that too disappeared as the temperature rose considerably. The walls of the tunnel now took on the appearance of porous grey sponge, hard and crystalline. Ahead, a dull red glow lit up the walls and every now and again a deep thunderous roar echoed up the tunnel.

He wondered if it was safe to go any further, but curiosity drove him on down the slope to where the tunnel opened out to a large cavern. The tunnel ended here, as the far wall ahead blocked any further progress quite apart from the fiery red glow which lit the whole place up like the inside of a furnace. The heat washed back from the walls threatening to set fire to anything which got too close.

He had to see what was going on in the huge pit ahead, and so slowly edged forward until he could look down onto the molten lava some fifty metres below. It seethed and bubbled like a living thing, and then suddenly began to rise up the huge tube. Some twenty metres from the top it now poured down a side tunnel and then the whole mass receded to its former level.

That which had gone down the side tunnel was now out of sight, but seconds later a deafening roar announced that something was coming up the shaft, and he leapt back to a safe distance, and only just in time.

With a deafening roar, a column of steam raced up the shaft and into a hole above.

If he had been any closer he would have been sucked into the mighty vortex and spewed out onto the planets surface, probably in little pieces. He was still shaking as he sat down back up the tunnel to contemplate what he had seen.

A faint nag had begun in his head, and not knowing if it was due to the heat or the call for another capsule, he guessed the latter, and set off back up the tunnel and things a little more familiar.

Looking into the shaft which housed the green slimy thing among the foliage, there was little to see, except the green drapes seemed to shiver a little and then lay still. Maybe it was still there and decided he was too big to tackle, for it had to eat something he reasoned.

Picking up the pile of hair-like threads he had left in the tunnel, his mind was already working on uses for it. If it could be spun into threads, then he could weave it into a crude cloth and make a carrying bag to transport the pods and crystals in much larger quantities than his arms could otherwise hold.

Half way back under the ice cliff there was a rushing noise and he froze on the spot. Several tonnes of ice fell off the cliff face, exposing bare rock and something which glinted as it was pushed along by the ice.

When all was still once more, he cautiously approached what appeared to be something which had been constructed rather than something which belonged to his world.

Despite it being still partly encased in ice, his claws soon removed the remainder to expose an ovaloid shape with what looked like a track driving system underneath. Protruding from a small turret on top of the device, a lens-like object looked forlornly at him.

Without even trying to think he instinctively knew it to be a robot probe, most likely sent down by those who had incarcerated him on this icy world.

Even as he watched, the once shiny metal surface turned grey as the protective ice had been removed, and a few moments later the little turret with the sad eye fell off.

How he knew what a probe was proved that his memory was returning of its own accord, stimulated by what he had seen and without any help from him digging into his past.

He longed to know if he had a name, but didn't dare look as he thought that would surely knock his head sideways, if the past searching was anything to go by.

The robot probe was falling to pieces as he watched, and he felt a little surge of pity for it, although it was only a machine. Something in the atmosphere didn't like alien entities paying uninvited visits.

Back in the cavern a capsule was speedily acquired and ingested, and a meal of pods helped down with the customary ice shards left him feeling his old self, the head pain slowly fading away.

As he relaxed, thoughts of thread making came up again, and he tried twisting a few strands together. When he released them, they sprang apart with a life of their own. And then he remembered, fold the twisted strands back on themselves and let go, the two strands then twist around each other. He tried it, and it worked.

It was not long before he had worked out that if one end of the threads was anchored to the ice wall, he could add more hair until he had reached the other side of the cavern, and then it was just a matter of keeping them separated with a block of ice until he had gone back to the start, and then released then.

Soon he had a large skein of thread ready for weaving into a crude cloth, but that would have to wait until he had replenished his stocks of food and crystals.

Life was almost enjoyable now, as long as he didn't try to remember the past and what might have been. Keep busy and beat the system, was his new motto, and so far it had seemed to work.

A slight nag in his head indicated that another capsule was needed, so how long had he been spinning? He had lost all track of time, although time meant little here as there was no means of measuring it, and no day or night.

Placing a crystal in the box, he waited for the mechanism to dispense his reward for so doing, and it dropped out of the slot at the bottom of the box. The slot snapped shut, and the lid would not now open. This meant it was time to take the box outside to the transporter rock, where it went up into the sky to later return for refilling.

Picking up the now fully loaded box, he made his way down the tunnel and out onto the ice sheet. New patches of bare ground had appeared in the ice since he was last outside, so this meant that the ice sheet was melting. This had never happened before, and he wondered if his cavern would eventually succumb to the melt, and then what would he do for shelter?

Bare ground was not so easy to travel on, although it might reveal more of the crystal containing rocks, but without softice there would be no food pods. Changes were taking place which he didn't understand, and he felt a little tingle of fear.

Placing the box on the black rock, he stood back as he had done so many times before and waited for the transporter to appear. A soft rushing noise announced its imminent arrival, and then the strange collection of struts and cylinders fell out of the sky and settled over the box. With a whoosh they both shot skywards, and he was left alone on the ice.

As he made his way back to the cavern he collected several crystals and a few pods from the fast disappearing softice pools, and with his arms fully loaded the need for something to carry things in if he had to travel greater distances for food, set his next task.

He felt quite tired by the time he had returned to the cavern, stacked his pods and crystals and had something to eat. He wondered about the yellow pods with the brown stripes, were they safe to eat? They smelled slightly aromatic, whereas the others didn't. As he already had one in his hand the temptation to try it was too much. He bit the end of the pod and let a little of the juice drip onto his tongue.

The aromatic smell now became stronger as his taste buds picked up the scent, and a sweetness, which was a new sensation to him, washed around his mouth.

With a look of surprise, he sat down up against the ice wall, just in case the juice had an adverse effect and he fell over. He was tempted to take a bite, but thought it better to allow some time to elapse before pushing his luck that far.

As he sat there waiting for something to happen, the thought of the carry bag came up again. He would have to try and weave a material of some kind, but was not sure where to begin.

Slowly his eyelids lowered, and he fell asleep to dream of 'materials' and an odd assortment of other unidentifiable things, but when he awoke some while later, he knew how he was going to make his cloth.

He would need a lot more of the strange hair-like substance, and as he felt no noticeable ill effects from the new pod juice, he ate a couple of the standard pods, checked to see if there was any hint of his head pain requiring a capsule, and set off for the tunnel under the cliffs.

There was now as much stony ground under the cliff as there was ice as the melt continued, and this slowed his progress a little, but the ice around the tunnel entrance seemed to be just as solid as before. Perhaps the sheer mass of it helps to keep it stable, he thought, and hoped it stayed that way.

As he passed the glowing crystal cave he felt strangely draw to enter it again, but then felt it was not quite the right time somehow.

Just before he reached the hair cave, he noticed a small hole in the tunnel wall on his left, and there was light behind it.

Peering through the hole he could see a large cave, lit by the yellow moss and what looked like a large collection of bones, but not bones as he remembered them.

The hole was not quite big enough for him to get his head in, but the thickness of the wall between the cave and the tunnel was only the width of his hand.

If only he had something to chip away the rock and enlarge the hole, he could fish out a few bones as he felt sure they would be useful. Fish....? He would come back armed with some thread and see if it was possible to get retrieve some.

The hair cave seemed to have recovered from his cropping of its contents, the new growth was nearly as long as that which surrounded it, so he didn't feel so bad about harvesting some more.

Depositing his haul in the tunnel, he wondered if there were any more caves he had missed as he had the bone cave in his first exploration, and resolved to be a little more observant in future.

The ground beneath his feet gave a shudder followed by a gush of air, and then it was still once more. Should he go on?

He waited, stock still to see what would happen next, but nothing did.

Cautiously he want on down the passageway to a point where the tunnel floor had collapsed into another cave, in the middle of which was a large hole and the sandy floor was still slowly trickling down to a level beneath. As all was quiet, except for the soft whisper of the sand, he thought it safe to enter.

The cave was larger than any he had seen before, and other caves lead off in all directions. It seemed as if there had been a large number of bubbles blown in the rock, and then he noticed a fine rain of sandy particles falling from above.

The mossy substance in this cave was giving out a much stronger light and therefore was more active, and then he solved the mystery of the caves.

Somehow, the strange moss spores must have found their way through fissures in the rock and began extracting the nourishment they needed, and in so doing caused it to disintegrate. The falling sand particles being the remains of the rock the moss had no use for or could not digest. In time the small cavity would grow into a much bigger one, the falling sand creating the floor.

He supposed in time the moss grew weaker, which explained why some caves had less light, and then would die out altogether, so leaving the cave in darkness.

Feeling pleased with his reasoning, he ventured a little further into the cave and looked down to where the sandy floor was disappearing. The hole was some five metres across, and he could see another cave beneath with a cone of sand building up under the hole.

The soft sound of the falling sand was joined by the steady rhythm of muffled footfalls, and one of the denizens of the lower caves came into view.

It was not something he would have liked to meet in the tunnel system, as the creature was composed of a large head with a beak like mouth, two spiteful black eyes and a short stumpy body on four sturdy legs. The apparition was about half his size, but looked twice as mean.

His weight must have caused an extra large fall of sand, and the creature looked up, opened its mouth exposing a fearsome set of razor-like teeth, and emitted a loud hiss.

Something the monstrosity had eaten could not have agreed with its digestive processes, as a waft of rancid decay drifted up to assail his nostrils.

Not wishing to show he had been intimidated by this display of unfriendliness, he quickly scooped a handful of sand down onto the creature's head. A muffled roar from 'foul breath' indicated its displeasure, and it backed down from the mound of sand causing it to flatten out. At least the hideous creature could no longer reach his level now, and he was thankful for that. The nightmare slowly shuffled away, and all was quiet again.

He realised that there may well be other caves beneath his feet, and thought it best to keep well away from the middle of any cave as this was the weakest point between the two levels.

A quick look around at the other caves showed one in which he could just see some colourful pod shapes hanging down from the roof, and carefully went over to investigate.

The roof of the cave was covered in groups of plant growth, between which the ubiquitous moss grew in great profusion.

Dangling from the plants were many pod-like growths, not unlike the ones in the softice pools, but brightly coloured.

Thinking they may be of some use, he plucked a few of each colour before retreating back to the tunnel to pick up the hair, and head back to the cavern.

On the way back he noticed the dull pain in his head calling for another capsule, and his anger arose once more at the way in which he had been entrapped in this system of pods and crystals. He would have to find some way out of it.

Storing the new pods in ice, he dropped another crystal into the ever hungry box, collected his capsule in the usual fumbling manner which only added to his anger, and sat down to think things over.

Of late he had seen many new things, extracted data from them, formed new ideas and increased his determinism to find a way of freeing himself from this never ending cycle of pain and forced work. If he could grow his own pods it would save the ever lengthening journey to the retreating ice field on the lower levels. 'The greatest bonus would be to free myself from the constantly reoccurring head pains and the damned crystals' he thought, as he munched on a pod. And then he remembered the striped pod.

The juice hadn't harmed him, so why not try eating one? He dug into the ice pile and extracted a small striped pod, and biting off the end he chewed it, enjoying the scented sweetness as it rolled around his mouth.

It was time to spin up some more thread so that the carry bag could be constructed, and he set about it with an enthusiasm, which when looking back, surprised him.

The pile of threads grew until he was out of hair to spin, and then he set about thinking of a way to weave the fabric for the bag.

Anchoring a line of threads to the wall of the cavern with small blocks of ice, he ran the other ends out towards the middle of the cave, locking them in place with ice blocks.

Now began the arduous task of weaving the cross threads, knotting each one to the warp as he went along. By the time he had woven a half metre, his fingers refused to work any more.

Remembering the capsule he had tried to preserve in its icy chamber, he went to have a look at it, and to his surprise it hadn't changed at all. He decided to take it next time he felt the need, and if it worked, he knew he would have gained another step towards his freedom. But freedom from what? The collecting cycle, yes, but what would he do with all the free time? Perhaps it was the feeling of being trapped.

He remembered the coloured pods, and thought it about time he had a look at them to see if they would be of any use.

One of them was a deep red, and not knowing quite why, dragged it across the surface of the ice wall, and now a deep red mark glistened on the otherwise pristine ice. Useful for a marker when I go exploring, he thought, and put it aside so that it didn't contaminate the other pods with its brilliant red dye.

A grey and green pod had somehow got squashed together, and where the juices had mixed they had set to a hard glue-like substance. This surprised, him, and he stood there hardly believing his luck, ideas racing through his mind in quick succession. Perhaps he could now stick things together, but first he would have to find things to stick, but what would he make?

A lone dark brown pod was as hard as the ice in the cavern wall, and showed no obvious use, but he kept it just the same.

By now, he would have expected a bit of a niggling pain in his head, but so far no sign of it. Perhaps he had got the time wrong. His fingers still felt as if they had been put through a mangle, but he gritted his teeth, and got on with the weaving.

Several cycles of fetching pods and crystals, feeding the collecting box interspersed with weaving his fabric, and the job was done. He stood back to admire his handiwork.

He now had the material to make his carry Bag, it was just a matter of folding it in half and tying the cross threads from each side together to complete the bag.

It only needed some form of strap so it could be hung from his neck, and he was ready to collect things in bulk. The platting of a wide band of threads took a little longer than he expected, but it was done and joined onto the bag.

And then the pain in his head began.

As yet it was only a nagging pain, but he could feel it increasing in severity as he tidied up the weaving equipment. Even the fact that he had succeeded in making his carry bag seemed to dim in importance as the pain relentlessly increased much quicker than it had ever done before.

As he reached for a crystal to put in the box, he then realised with shock how long it had been since he had done so. He now had a full blown eye watering raging head ache.

A thought was forming at the back of his mind, but he couldn't quite get it, something to do with the pods....and then it was gone.

The crystal went in, the capsule came out and after the usual fumbling, he put it into his mouth, still feeling a bit confused.

This time was different, it burnt his tongue as it burst, but before he could spit it out the contents had trickled down his throat, and a wave of nausea swept through him. Within seconds his legs didn't seem to belong to him any more, he could hardly control them as he staggered towards the ice wall of the cavern.

The light was slowly fading out to a dull greyness and a persistent ringing noise sang in his head as his body slumped down to the ice floor in an untidy heap. He could still feel his body, but it wouldn't respond when he tried to move it.

Slowly, blackness descended like an all enveloping blanket, cutting out his vision and soaking up even the faintest sounds from his world. Was he dreaming?

It didn't seem like a dream, it was too real. That awful stretching feeling again, he was being pulled out like a piece of elastic to span halfway across the universe, and when he felt he must surely break in two.....snap....he was back in one piece again.

Two:
The Transfer Unit

He was aware of being on his back because of the dull grey light above him, but he couldn't see any details of his surroundings, or feel any part of his body. He tried to move, but nothing happened. If he had limbs, they didn't respond.

There was just the sensation of being suspended in something, and a general woolliness. He was neither hot nor cold, there was no motion or sound... he just was.

And then he could hear the soft only just audible whirring of machinery to his right which was accompanied by a blazing white light which burned down on him unmercifully through his closed eyelids, causing him to scream out in pain, but there was no sound.

Slowly the irises closed down to mere pinpoints cutting out the blast of light to a bearable level, and the pain lessened.

A lukewarm fluid was being dripped onto his eyelids, and as it dissolved the sticky mucus which had sealed his eyes shut for so long, some of it crept under the now loosened lids causing another almost unbearable rush of pain.

Gradually the stinging eased off, and he felt a swab being gently worked across his eyelids, this was then followed by another squirt of some fluid, and his eyes opened.

Above him there seemed to be a mass of complicated machinery, pipes, cables, indicators and general confusion.

Where the hell am I? Was a rhetorical thought rather than a direct question as he couldn't vocalise. Below him something was in constant motion, but only just discernable, like a series of gentle waves rippling beneath him in a random pattern. He felt he was floating or being supported on something that was alive.

'Ah, you're back with us, welcome! Just in case you've forgotten, don't try to move, because you can't. The support system has taken care of your body while you were away, and it will take a little time for you to regain control again.'

'The Orientater will be with you in just a little while.' The disembodied voice moved away and he was left in the company of the many and varied mechanical devices which had looked after his needs for so long. The feeling of panic rose in his throat like a scalding hot liquid and he fought to retain some semblance of sanity.

He hardly heard the soft double click of a valve opening and closing as a warm tingling sensation swept through his body, the lights dimmed and he drifted into a gentle sleep.

When he came to, there was one of the little two legged people sitting beside him. He couldn't see the legs, but recognised the head and shoulders from his dreams.

'Hello Brandon, I am your Orientater, and it is my job to put you at ease, to take away your fears and explain things to you. You will be unable to speak for a while as your larynx has not been used for a long time, so therefore the cords have lost their ability to produce sound. You do have control of your eyelids, so you can indicate yes and no by blinking once for yes, and twice for no. Do you understand?'

Blink.

'Good, now I will try and set your mind at rest about the situation you are in. We don't know how much you will remember from your past, so I will tell you a little about it. But first of all, you're in good hands, you are well and you can come to no harm here. Do you understand?'

Blink.

'Ok, you have a body just like mine, but you will not be able to feel it or make it work for a while, but do not worry, the support system takes care of everything, probably better than you could. Your body has been in a deep coma for a long time, while you have been somewhere else. You will remember some of your experiences as thought they were a dream, but in fact they were real.'

'You have been occupying a body on another world, in fact we are in the space station orbiting that world right now. The body you've been in is quite safe in an ice cave, and is in a deep sleep, as your body was here until a short time ago. Do you follow me so far?'

Blink.

'Do you feel disorientated or afraid of being here?'

Blink, Blink.

'Good, I can assure you all is well, and you are in safe hands here, in time you will regain your ability to speak to us, and I look forward greatly to that. You do not need to eat or drink, the equipment takes care of all your bodily needs, and much more.

You may have noticed that there is a feeling of movement beneath you, that is the body suspension unit massaging your back so that you don't get compression sores, and also helping your circulation. Once, long ago, I tried it and found it most a pleasurable experience, do you like it Brandon?'

Blink.

'That's good, Brandon, I'm glad you feel comfortable, Now for a few more details. You may or may not remember your life down there on the planet, but you have been collecting purple crystals for us. They are very valuable, and you have amassed a great fortune in credits. When your body has fully recovered you will be able to have anything you want. You are far more wealthy than all of us put together, and then some. Isn't that great?'

Pause...Blink.

'It's good to have you back with us Brandon, and we look forward to you telling us all about your adventures later on. I think it's now time for you to take another little rest while your body gets back to normal, but I will be here when you awaken again, so don't worry'.

The soft click of some hidden piece of equipment, and the world of Bran faded into nothingness again.

This time the dreams returned. He was up on the higher ice plateau and had travelled many hundreds of kilometres towards the dark Blue Mountains which fringed the horizon.

With boundless energy he galloped along, sending a flurry of ice chips in all directions as he sped towards the massive rock formations ahead. The higher up the long slope he went, the thinner the air became, but it didn't seem to affect him, much to his surprise. Clambering up the final ridge of rocks, he looked down on a valley of green lushness, the like of which he could have only imagined.

Trees many times his height were laden with brightly coloured fruiting pods towering over bushes of multi coloured berries. Soft velvety grass carpeted the ground in all direction as far as the eye could see, while a little silver stream wound in and out of the rocky clusters which dotted the valley bottom.

From his vantage point, he looked down in wonder at what lay before him, and then he was among the plants and trees, eating the fruits and berries in the gentle warmth of a clear blue sky. Stopping to drink freely at a pool which adjoined the stream, he saw his reflection in the clear water and could not help but admire the perfect physique before him.

He never really thought of himself as handsome, and it came as quite a shock to see himself so clearly portrayed in the crystal clear waters. With free water dripping from his soft velvety muzzle, he raised his head to take in the sweetly scented air

The sky above grew dark, the light dimming all around him while colours faded into shades of grey and black. The sound of the tinkling stream was no more, and then there was nothingness….

'Hello Bran, it's me again. Hope you had a good rest, you've been asleep for ages. We have a problem, the monitors tell us that your vocal cords will not respond to stimuli, and therefore may not work correctly again. Would you be very concerned about this?'

Blink.

'We are very sorry about this, and will do all we can to restore your larynx to normal, but at the moment we can't guarantee it. If we have to, would you be willing to for us to operate surgically on you?'

Blink.

'Thank you Bran, we understand this must be very disappointing for you, but we will do our best. Now, we have a question we would like to get an answer to, and that's why is there sometimes a delay in returning the crystal collecting box? Do you understand the question?'

Blink, Blink.

There was no way he was going to tell them a damn about it, or anything else if he could help it. He wasn't sure why, but he didn't trust them one centimetre. There was something deceitful going on, but as yet he couldn't figure out exactly what it was.

They weren't telling him the whole story by a very long chalk, so he wasn't going to volunteer any information which might weaken his hand in the future.

It was plain to see not only disappointment, but sheer naked frustration on the face of the Orientater, and that just confirmed his suspicions about the whole setup.

Why had they asked him if he minded if they operated on his larynx? There was nothing he could do about it if they wanted to, so why ask? They were misdirecting his attention from something, but what? They were withholding something, and he needed to know just what it was.

'Were you having difficulty in finding enough crystals sometimes Bran?' That was safe enough to answer, and should allay any suspicions they may have about him holding back information, as they had no way of knowing what really happened on the planet, he thought.

Using a mixture of non understanding and innocence, he reckoned to mislead them until he could figure out just what it was they were withholding from him.

Obviously they had no visual means of observing what he was up to on his home world, as he now thought of it, so he could lie with impunity as long as he remembered what he had said before, and didn't contradict it the future.

'Was the ice around your cave melting just before you came back here?' Bran didn't answer as he felt the question being asked was a mask for something else they wanted to know. 'Can you recall if the conditions on the planet were changing before you came back?' Got a negative answer.

If they didn't know, he certainly wasn't going to tell them, let them think he was a lot dumber then he really was. He would have to be very careful what he said 'yes' and 'no' to in the future, as they could no doubt find out a lot more about him and what he had been up to by rephrasing the questions carefully, and getting information by implication.

In a way, he would rather be down on the planet than here, at least he could move around and do more or less what he chose there. Here he was trapped in a body which he couldn't move, and somehow doubted if it ever would, although some sensation was coming back in his legs it was small compensation for being able to roam about as he chose.

'I think it would be wise for you to have another little rest now Bran, and I'll be back to talk to you later.'

Blink.

Well, that's got rid of him, Bran thought, although he did consider the 'rest' was not necessarily meant for him. Very slowly sensation was coming back to his body, and he looked forward to sitting up and taking a good look around the room, as he was sure there would be a lot of information to be gleaned from that, and a clue to his future perhaps.

There were several more visits from the Orientater, although he didn't do much 'orientating', it was just a series of very cleverly phrased questions to ferret out as much information from Bran as possible with regards to conditions on the planet, and how Bran really felt about crystal collecting.

He didn't give very much away, pretending to not understand the more probing questions, and feigning lack of memory on others that might be too revealing in their answers.

Bran remembered the 'day-night' 'light-dark' concept he had come up with back home, but there was no evidence of it here, although he did notice that people seemed to come and go in shifts, and very few even looked at him.

He was beginning to feel like a piece of the damned machinery itself, for he got no more attention paid to him than it did.

Funny that, I still consider the ice world my home, he thought, and now longed to return to it.

There were more visits from the 'Inquisitor' as Bran like to think of him, and a few from some technicians, or so he supposed, as they didn't ask him anything, only looking at the instruments and talking in low voices among themselves.

They were a miserable lot in his eyes, totally ignoring him as a person and alluding to various functions in short staccato tones full of scientific jargon, arrogantly assuming he would not know what they were referring to.

As time went by, Bran became more convinced than ever that they were not really interested in him at all.

This was brought home to him when a new bunch of 'Techs' came bustling into the room and began altering the equipment, making some new additions and taking some items away. Not one of them spoke to him, or even looked him in the eye, he was just an extension of the equipment, and was expected to function along with it, their interest only perked up if things looked as if they were going wrong.

Having no idea of how much time had passed since he had been returned to the Orbiter, Bran was getting to hate the place with a deep loathing which bordered on the unhealthy, and would have given anything to go home to his cosy ice cavern.

Perhaps they would send him back again, and he bitterly regretted not being able to speak to them. During one shift there was a great commotion among the personal as several high ranking personages with lots of gold braid on their uniforms came into the room to see him and the equipment.

Bran blinked his eyes furiously to try and attract their attention and communicate the fact that he was a living being with feelings. It was a total waste of time and not a considerable amount of effort, as they hardly looked at him, let alone made any attempt to talk, and the final insult was when in muted tones they referred to him as 'it'.

It was at this point Brad made up his mind to terminate all co-operation, except that which might return him to his own world. He had had enough of the farce which was going on around him, coupled with the fact that his body was still in a state of paralysis as far as he was concerned, some sensation having returned to his limbs, but no motive power.

He was now among those who had sent him to the ice world in the first place, and far from wanting to seek revenge on them, he wanted to go back to what he thought of as his world more than anything he could think of.

Eventually the High Brass left along with the rest of the crew, some of which had very red faces and didn't look at all happy. Bran had the feeling that all was not well for some of his keepers, and hoped they would not take it out on him.

He noticed that every four shifts there was a long wait before anyone else came into the room, and he was left entirely on his own for that time. In vain he tried to move his arms and legs, but nothing worked, even his breathing was done for him by a machine and he was left to lay there and think the worst.

It was during one of these 'alone' times that the Visitor came. Bran had closed his eyes, and was trying to get into a dream state of his ice world, when he noticed a small dark figure had come into the room and was standing beside the device in which he lay.

The Visitor was very old and had long white hair which flowed down to his shoulders, where it swept around to the back of his neck and was tied together in a bunch. His face was kindly and wise looking with fine features, not like the 'robots' which normally tended Bran's needs. He wished he could speak, as the Visitor just stood there motionless, saying nothing.

At last the Visitor spoke. 'I understand that you can hear but not speak, and you can answer yes or no by blinking your eyes.'

Blink, from Bran.

'Good, I have a lot to tell you, and only a few hours to tell it in. It is a long story, which began with fine high ideals and has ended with deceit, treachery, greed and a total disregard for our fellow creatures.'

Bran somehow knew this man was nothing to do with the Orientater, or any of the rest of the team, and was perhaps on his side.

'I am sickened by what I have seen and heard, and am powerless to prevent this disgraceful and disgusting trade in suffering from continuing into the future. I feel free to tell you, as I know you can't repeat this to anyone, and I feel that you should at least know the truth of what has happened to you and others of your kind. Have you understood me so far?'

Bran replied with a slow but definite blink.

'Good, I must go back many years to give you the basics on which the whole operation was structured in the beginning. I was a very young man, with fine ideals and a trust in my fellow beings. If I had known then what I know now, I would rather have died than contributed to the cruelty that has been perpetrated against my fellow beings, and I feel largely responsible for a lot of it through my ignorance of so called human nature.

It all began, when fresh out of the Academy and with my research grant firmly in my pocket, I looked around for a subject of interest to work on.

One day, someone brought me a paper on 'out of body' experiences, and that was it. Please be patient, it is most important that you understand the significance of this.

The research papers listed many accounts of people who, under anaesthetic or enforced bodily unconsciousness, were able to see and hear things which were happening around them.

This sometimes happens in operating theatres of hospitals and in traumatic accidents. There have been many cases of this kind of thing happening going back through history for a very long time, but it has always been considered a 'fringe' type of thing, and never taken seriously by the scientific community. Am I going too fast for you?'

Blink, Blink.

'Good, I will continue. If I say something which you do not understand, please blink three times, and I will try and elaborate for you. Do you understand?'

Blink.

'The paper we were working on referred to the 'human psyche', the soul, unit of awareness, that which is aware of being aware, the real you, not the bodies we are in or use. Many religions say we have a soul, but they have got it wrong, you don't have a soul, you are one. Do you understand this concept?'

Blink.

'Yes, of all people, you will understand this very well, how silly of me to ask. To continue, we found someone who was able under certain conditions to exteriorise from his body and see things in another room, make a note of it, and tell us about it upon returning to his body.

We made the test more and more difficult, so that any chance of trickery or cheating was impossible, as we had to have conclusive proof of the phenomenon. We found several people who were able to exteriorise from their bodies at will over the years that followed, but it was the next stage that was to lead to the present situation.

We called people with this ability 'extrans', *ex* to represent the exteriorisation and *trans* for movement or travel. We had to call them something. Quite by accident on day, one of our '*extrans*' reported that he had momentarily taken over a body which was in a coma and caused it to move and speak.

When we checked up on this, we found it to be true and the hospital was in turmoil. It would seem from later research that a coma is when a 'person' leaves their body, for whatever reason, and the body seems to go into a deep sleep. As long as bodily functions are kept going by a support system, the body, albeit in a coma, will continue to live.

'Am I going too fast?' asked the Visitor.

Blink, Blink.

'Ok, the idea of a person being able to take over another body, if in a coma, was too much to pass up, so we spent a lot of time trying to set up experiments to see if anything could be gained by it.

The whole thing fell apart when it was found that a 'taken over' body had a completely different set of memories and a different personality. That proved our findings beyond all possible doubt, and then the troubles began.

Someone, somewhere, felt threatened, possibly as this could disprove hard held beliefs, or it threatened their power in some way. We were told in no uncertain terms to close down any more research, and go our separate ways. And so the project was put on hold, as far as we knew.

Some years later I was offered a plumb job to do some research in space physics, and I accepted of course, little knowing at the time what it was to entail.

Basically, a planet had been found with an almost impossible set of circumstances. It had a very high gravity, and circled a pair of suns, each in turn, which orbited around each other.

Because of the unusual nature of the system, a probe was sent down to explore, take measurements, and bring back samples. One of the samples was a large deep purple crystal.

Why this caused such a stir, we didn't know, but the dive was on to get more, whatever the cost, and the total cost was unimaginably high.

More probes were sent, most of which never returned, and then it was discovered that the planet's atmosphere was incredibly corrosive to all our materials, and a probe only lasted a very short while, which was evident from the few which did make it back to the Orbiter.

'Eventually, after all attempts to retrieve the crystals failed, someone suggested trying to recover some organic material from the planet, and through genetic engineering, construct a creature which could do the collecting, as it would be impervious to the corrosive atmosphere.

I know it seems impossible, but they went ahead and somehow succeeded. It was at this point I was called in, the *Extrans* files reopened, and the rest is history.

I don't want to bore you with all the petty detail, but the upshot of it was to try and get a 'person' to take over the body of the animal they had created.

Many attempts failed, but at last they got it right, and you were the first person to achieve this unholy bonding and survive.

I am so sorry, Bran. I had no idea it would turn out as it has, with such ruthlessness and disregard for human life. When it was realised that I was so against continuing the project, I was removed from any active part of it, and could only watch on in growing horror and dismay.

A zircon based glass was developed which could withstand the atmosphere of the planet for a short while, and probes were coated with this extending their life a little.

Using these new probes, they managed to retrieve enough plant and animal material to construct the creature you inhabit on the planet's surface.

A mind block was installed so that once in the creature, you could not recall who or what you really were, and if you tried, you got a painful jolt for your troubles.

Somehow you had to be locked into the crystal retrieving cycle, and they did this by convincing you that only one type of food pod was edible, and it just happened that it lacked a certain mineral you needed to survive. Without it your body would experience extreme pain.

By putting a crystal in the collecting box, you got a capsule which contained the necessary mineral which then relieved the pain. It was at this point that I objected to what they were doing, and I was removed from the project. It was too late, there was nothing I could do to help you.

I don't know how long you can survive the mental and physical pressures you are under, and they realise this too.

The vast zircon tank your creature body was made in, is now growing another, and a female has been found with your abilities. So far I don't think she realises just what is entailed, and I can't get to warn her.

She will be sent down one of these days, but I don't know when. If you survive long enough, you may be able to meet up with her, and so have a little company, but this is only supposition on my part. I don't really think they will allow you both to exist at the same time somehow, it could lessen their control of the situation.

I have talked long enough, and the shift is about to change over so I had better go. I will try and visit you again, and give you any information I think that will help you survive.

Once again, Bran, I am so very sorry for my part in getting you into such a terrible situation.'

The Visitor's voice was breaking, and Bran felt sorrier for him than he did for himself. The old man shuffled out of the room, closing the door quietly behind him.

Shortly after the Visitor left, the next shift of technicians came in with their usual insular and arrogant attitude towards him.

A new piece of equipment was wheeled in and attached to Bran's survival machine. Cables were plugged in, switches switched, and dials lit up followed by a loud bang, and then all the lights went out.

The ensuing pandemonium was something to behold.

Bran looked forward to their next attempt to install the new equipment, but then began to worry in case it was vital to his survival, as his body wasn't recovering as he had been told it should, but then again he was getting used to being lied to.

While he was still mulling over the latest developments, there was a soft click from somewhere within the machine, his eyelids closed and he slipped into oblivion once again.

Dreams came and went, but one frightened him more than most. He was hitched up to a machine with cables, wires and tubes which somehow connected him to something else, but he couldn't see what.

'Are you ready?' asked a masked face, a switch was thrown and he felt fear as he had never done before. He tried to get up but his body was numb, he had no muscle control. He tried to call out, but no sound issued. The stretching feeling began almost at once and he was looking out of a huge tank at a lot of odd looking little people on two legs, who were jumping about in great jubilation.

He tried to move, but he seemed to be in thick treacle, the fluid giving way to his massive limbs very slowly and great effort was needed just to lift his head a little. Although the fluid and the glass tank distorted his view, he could see all the equipment and a table on which lay one of the little people, hitched up in a spider's web of wires and tubes. He then realised it was him, but he was in the tank.

One of the little people was remonstrating violently to the others, and then ran over to the table, did something, and stretch....... he was back in his body.

The technicians crowed around him in great excitement. 'It's alright, you made the transfer, well done.' When he got his voice back he hoarsely said 'Please, I don't want to do it again, it's an awful sensation.' He was begging for his very existence.

'You'll get used to it in time,' said one of the masked technicians, 'anyway, we've put too much into this to stop now.' The dream faded and a restful sleep took over, but he remembered most of it when he awoke to the sounds of frenzied activity.

Some new equipment was wheeled in and connected to Bran's support unit, the lights came on and there was no accompanying explosion, much to his disappointment. A group of high ranking officials joined the others, who were now standing to rigid attention.

One of the officials leaned over the prone form of Bran, and with a twisted grin swung one of the instrument panels across on its gimbals, so that Bran could see a reflection of himself in the highly polished surface.

'Take a good look before we send you down again.' He was not ready for what he saw. A very old man gazed back at him with tired rheumy eyes, a skin which was wrinkled almost to obscenity and covered in discoloured blotches. A saggy skinned bony skeleton lay in a disordered heap within the pristine life support unit.

Someone barked an order, a switch was thrown and he felt a faint vibration from somewhere deep within the support unit. The dreadful stretching began. This time he tried to experience the sensation rather than resist it, and snap he was back home in his ice cavern.

Bran tried to open his eyes, but they were glued shut. A careful probe with a fingernail removed some of the mucus which had dried to a hard crust, and he could see again. Was it all a bad dream?

He tried to remember what he had been doing just before awakening, and stopped himself just in time. A picture of the Orbiter control room hazily formed, and then grew in clarity.

The pictures got brighter and they were all there, the technicians, the high rankers and especially the one with the cruel grin. The awful shock he got when he saw himself reflected in the instrument panel.

Bran realised that if he was careful he could extract a lot of data from his memory, just as long as he didn't dig too deep and trigger the pain pulse.

He had gained a little more control over the situation as he now had access to a good supply of food, plenty of crystals and the ability to gain a little more information about himself and the situation in general.

He could determine when he sent the crystals up, and if he could preserve the food pods and maybe the capsules, he was free to explore his world instead of the tightly controlled cycle of the past.

His main worry was what would happen to him if his body back on the Orbiter died, and that seemed inevitable. Considering how he had seen himself, that could be sooner rather than later, and he felt a flush of fear.

Were they ready to send down the next creature complete with the poor sod who would be trapped in it as he was? And would he be able to make contact, that's if she survived? He decided to not worry over things he couldn't control, and attend to the present.

He was hungry, and staggered over to the pile of ice chips which had preserved his food pods. Gulping down four in quick succession, with the inevitable belch or two, he saw the striped pods and then remembered the last time he had eaten one there seemed to be a delay in the pain returning after the last capsule he had taken. It was worth a try, and two of the striped pods joined the others he had already ingested. Maybe these pods contained the minerals the Visitor had mentioned.

Still feeling stiff from his long sleep and a little unsteady on his legs, he made his way out of the tunnel and into the outside world.

The massive glacier in which his cavern had been formed was still intact, but looking a little dirty and showing signs of breaking up around the edges. The ice field had retreated into the far distance and he was now surrounded by hard stony ground, although the upper ice sheet still hung over the massive cliff dividing his world in two. He remembered what the Visitor had said about the planet changing suns, and hoped the return of the ice field would be soon so that he could get back to a relatively normal life.

In the distance he could see several lumps of the red crystal bearing rock, and returned to the cavern to get his carry bag, as now would be a good time to stock up on crystals before the ice returned and covered everything up again.

There were no softice pools in sight, and that meant no food pods, so he would have to make a long journey to reach the retreating ice sheet and hoped pods grew there.

Bran laboured long and hard to build his stocks up, and blessed the day he thought of making the carry bag. What other treasures did the caves under the mountains hold?

The bone cave came to mind, and he wondered how he could enlarge the hole in the cave wall so he could get at the bones.

His aching limbs refused to go down to the ice sheet again, so he had a good meal and curled up for a much needed rest.

The dreams began almost at once, and for the first time he didn't feel frightened by their content, although some made him angry in his dream. His sleep deepened, the dreams faded away and sonorous snores echoed around the ice cavern for a long time as his huge body recovered form the arduous tasks he had asked of it.

Feeling much refreshed after his long sleep, Bran ate a hearty meal, put a crystal in the collecting box, stored the capsule in its ice container against possible need, and with his carry bag around his neck, set off for the tunnel under the mountain.

He had added a few pods, a chunk of ice and some of his home made thread to the bag, so that his needs for the expedition were well covered.

The lack of a capsule being taken before he left caused him a little worry, but he felt fairly confident that the striped pods he had eaten held the necessary minerals to prevent the pain returning.

He found it hard going under the ice cliff, as the lower ice sheet had retreated so far, but to go down to the ice and then return would have made his journey unbearably long, and he wanted to explore as much as possible before he had to return to his ice cave.

As he approached the tunnel entrance, he noticed a little further along a massive fall of ice from the upper ice sheet, and saw a glint of what looked like metal. What looked like a huge box, still buried in the ice block had one face exposed, and was showing signs of corrosion.

Bran approached with the usual caution to find what appeared to be a large door, hinged from the bottom. He gave one exposed edge a tug and the whole thing moved a little, but not enough for him to see inside.

Repeated attempts loosened the remainder of the ice which was holding the door in place, and it came crashing down with an enormous thud. The inside was dark and a foul stale smell assaulted his nostrils as he bent forward to peer inside.

As his eyes accustomed themselves to the low light level, he could see a great web like structure in the centre of the box within which hung a huge fabric bag.

Swirls of fine powder arose about his feet as he slowly moved up to the bag-like container, and gripping an edge, gave it a tug. It fell into shreds, showering him in dust to reveal a nightmare he would remember for a long time.

Suspended in a harness of webbing was a replica of himself, gaunt and dried out, but still recognisable. At some time in the past, they had sent down a creature to forage for crystals, and the landing craft had fallen into a cleft in the ice, and as the door was unable to open the whole thing had got covered in from the storms, and lay buried until the ice cliff had fallen.

The eyes were dead, but had a pleading look about them, something he would never forget. Bran shuddered at what the poor creature must have gone through before it had died in agony from dehydration, or maybe the shock of landing had been merciful and killed it outright.

Finding the Lander and its sad occupant left him in a melancholy mood as he made his way back to the tunnel and into the bowels of the mountain.

As he passed the crystal cave he looked in, and somehow felt drawn towards it. He went in, and almost immediately the crystals seemed to glow extra brightly, and he had a sensation of floating, as if he wasn't really there, but where was he? And then the feeling was no more, and he found the sadness had gone too.

Reaching the hole in the wall of the bone cave, Bran looked in and saw that it was just as he had seen it before.

Nothing had been added or moved, so he felt a little better about raiding its contents for his own use, although he wasn't sure just what that use was at the moment.

Attaching a pod to a length of his cord to give it some weight, Bran threw it through the hole in the wall and heard a hollow clatter from within as the bones were disturbed.

After many frustrating attempts, he succeeded in fishing out a bone, but it was like no other bone he had ever seen. It had a metallic feel about it and was very heavy for its size.

About one metre long, one end had a round knob on it, while the other tapered to a fine point. Bran stood there puzzled for a moment. How can a pointed bone join up with another one? He wondered, but there was no answer to that.

Holding the bone like a dagger, he began to chip away at the thin wall which separated him from the bone cave. When the hole was big enough for him to get his head in, he did so, and was surprised to see the cave was joined up to many others, but only this one seemed to have bones. Then he saw something which would make his job easier. Out of reach, but within throwing distance of his lasso, was a large club-like bone. Both arms ached from the continual pounding at the wall, and then he realised that he was ambidextrous, while in his old body he was right handed.

After a short rest and a meal of pods washed down with ice chips from the block in his carry bag, it was time to bring the hammer bone into action, driving the pointed end of the other bone deep into the rock. It made a great difference, and whole chunks of the thin wall gave way to his energetic pounding.

Having made the hole big enough for him to squeeze through at a pinch, the thought crossed his mind that anything within the caves which wanted to get out, could now do so. He would have to go in and try to find some bones large enough to block the hole.

As he moved around in the cave he was making far more noise among the clattering bones that he thought was prudent, there was no point in advertising his presence here.

There was little he could do about it as they were so dense they almost rang like a bell when struck.

Having punched out a row of five holes down one side of the opening, he then chiselled a matching series of angled groves in the other, and after much fiddling about, he found bones which he could push into the holes and slot into the grooves.

Nothing can get them out unless it has the intelligence to lift them out of the grooves first, he thought, and stood back to admire his handiwork.

Now to the business of selecting the ones he wanted, but what were they? A collection of the dagger-like bones were deposited outside in the tunnel and then he looked around for inspiration. The idea of a sledge came to mind, and a collection of suitable bones were located, and they joined the others in the tunnel.

Bran felt he had done enough for one day, to use a now meaningless term, and gathered up as many bones as he could into his bag, with the other larger ones held firmly under his arms.

By the time he had returned to his cavern, he was exhausted, and sank down in a heap against the ice wall. Recovering after a while, he thought it time to put another crystal into the box, and stored the capsule in the ice block along with the others.

The striped pods seem to be working, he thought to himself, as here was no sign of the expected head pain. Still tired, but mentally active, Bran thought about the sledge.

He had the bones, and hair to bind them together, but would that be strong enough? The pods which glued themselves together suggested a possible solution of strengthening the joints, and he located one of each, and bound two bones together with hair. He squeezed the juice from each pod into an empty husk, mixed it with a tuft of hair bound onto a small thin bone, painting the mixture onto the joint.

The mixture seemed to thicken as he watched, and before long the bones were locked together as one. The building of the sledge took several 'days', and a few trips for more hair and glue pods, which were not quite as numerous as the other types.

Once completed, he made a harness from platted hair cord and was now ready to try out his creation. The sledge dragged on the hard stony ground, but once on the ice, it ran smoothly.

Locating some of the red crystal bearing rocks was easy, as all the protecting ice had gone. After the sledge was loaded with crystals, he bound them in place with cord and set off for his cavern and a well earned rest.

The next time a crystal was placed in the collecting box, the lid snapped shut, as did the bottom slot. Time to send 'em another load, he thought, and then hesitated.

If he delayed each delivery a little, it would give the impression that either he was getting weak, or crystals were getting scarce. In time, he would smear a little blood on a few crystals before he sent them to give the impression he was injured, and this might focus their minds upon sending his replacement, although he was not sure if it might bring about his demise at the same time.

If his replacement came, and he was now sure they would do anything to make this happen once he looked as if he was failing, how could he communicate to her? He had tried to speak, but only got a muted roar for is troubles. He would have to practice until he succeeded, unless he had no vocal cords as such.

The first few attempts dampened his hopes, but he persisted until he managed to make a few words resemble human speech to some slight degree, but would they be good enough?

Another problem came to mind when he was resting after a hard days collecting. If he was to go looking for the green valley of his dreams, he would have to find a way of preserving the food pods, for if left outside the ice pile, they just dried out slowly, going to seed, and became inedible.

The fire chamber seemed a good idea. If he could string them up in the warm air flow they should dry out before they could go to seed.

But first he would have to construct another carry bag, and go down to the edge of the fast disappearing ice sheet to get a really large stock of pods. Having made one bag and solved the problems of so doing, the second one took less time, but was just as labour intensive.

The job was done, and he set off in high spirits with both bags and the sledge. The softice pools were becoming harder to find, but he managed to fill both bags, pick up a few more crystals, and headed for home.

As the collecting box was ready for dispatch, and he thought he had delayed it's sending long enough to indicate that things were getting a little difficult, he carried it out to the rock and left it for the carrier to come down and take it up to the Orbiter.

A small bag was constructed from the remains of his hair stock to carry ice chips for the trip to the fire chasm, as there had been no sign of water within the tunnels, except for the cave with the green slimy thing slithering about in the green drapes, and he didn't fancy drinking that somehow.

Armed with his ice bag, the big carry bag containing several dagger-like bones, a few lengths of cord and the pods for drying, he set of for the fire chasm. The crystal cave was shining like a beacon, and he felt strangely linked to it somehow, the Hair cave had re grown its hair and was ready for cropping again.

Water still poured down the centre of the green growth cave, but there was no sign of 'slimy', so Bran stood there for a while breathing in the cool damp air and feeling much refreshed from it.

The long slope down to the fire chasm still puzzled him, as the sound of the lava pump was hardly discernible until he was well into the main cavern. Perhaps the porous rock walls absorbed the sound, but it still didn't seem right.

Putting his bags down well away from the main heat source, Bran set about driving the pointed bones into the walls of the cavern, and then joined them up with the cord.

Several times he had to retreat to the back of the cavern as the mighty lava pump pulsed up the shaft and then withdrew to regain its strength, while the superheated steam screamed up the shaft to the outside world.

A nip from his teeth left a small cut in the end of each pod which was then hung on the cords to dry. Bran took a rest at the back of the cavern to eat and chew on the ice chips, as the heat had dehydrated him somewhat. His thick coat was designed for a much cooler place, he mused. The pods were gently swaying in the warm air flow and Bran though as there was little more for him to do down here, he would return to the coolness of the ice world he was used to.

On the way back, he stopped at the green cave, attached a food pod to a piece of cord and dangled it through the opening to see what, if anything, would happen. He was about to give up when there was vicious tug on the cord, and it went limp. When he pulled it in, the cord had been severed cleanly where it had been attached to the pod. He decided to treat the cave with a little more respect in future, those teeth were sharp.

As he left the tunnel he noticed a thick mist rolling up from the lower ice sheet towards the cliffs.

Was the cool time returning? He hoped so, as it was hard work pulling the sledge over the stony ground, and it would wear out the runners if he wasn't careful. Half way back to the cavern he realised the wind had picked up, and was driving the long tendrils of mist ever closer, and they were thickening. A flicker of lightning high above increased his pace, he didn't want to be caught out in a storm.

By the time he had reached his cavern, the first few flurries of ice crystals were in the air. the clouds had thickened, and a distant rumble of thunder foretold of a full blown storm on the way. The ice was coming back.

Bran dumped his carry bags in the entrance of the tunnel, and hurried over to the launch rock to retrieve the collecting box. He was tired, and after a quick meal, curled up to sleep a well deserved sleep, the day had gone well. and he had achieved all he had set out to do.

The storm raged and pounded the outside world, but Bran was oblivious to the cacophony of sounds as ice laden air roared up the cliffs to deposit its load on the upper ice sheet, replacing that which had been ripped away during the warm up. Eventually the storm died down and a strange stillness pervaded Bran's area of the planet.

Suddenly he was awake, not just awakened, but wide awake, and he leapt to his feet in anticipation of possible trouble. Something was different, he looked around and everything seemed to be the same, the pods resided in their ice pile, the collecting box lay where he had put it. His hair stocks hung from a bone driven into the ice wall. So what was so different?

And then he knew. He felt free, really free, it was as if a weight had been lifted from his shoulders and he was the lighter for it. He sat down with a thump. It had happened, and he had survived.

High above in the orbiting space station, a technician was reading a report when out of the corner of his eye he saw a change in the usual pattern of signals on the monitor.

One of the usually bumpy lines had now gone flat, and a red light was blinking. He hit the panic button far harder than was necessary, and the piercing shriek of the 'something has gone horribly wrong' alarm sounded.

Within seconds three high grade Techs rushed in, grabbed the heart stimulator and applied it to the crumpled form in the support tank. The pathetic little bundle of skin and bones jerked grotesquely several times, but remained lifeless and still when they removed the device.

'Poor sod's gone,' one of them commented, 'better tell the Chief.' There was little ceremony as they tipped the sad remains of a once happy, healthy man in his thirties, into a disposal sack, and threw it into the chute to the incinerator.

Phase two of the crystal gathering operation would now have to be pushed forward a little sooner than anyone really wanted. Someone was likely to suffer horribly.

When Bran recovered from the shock of what had happened he could hardly believe it. Was he really free from those above? He certainly felt different.

He tried to recall what had happened on the space station, and the pictures came flooding in with no sharp stab of pain in is head.

The next problem was to get ready for the new crystal gatherer, as he felt sure it would be sent soon if the crystals failed to arrive on time. He must delay the crystal sending accordingly, so that things were not too rushed at their end, so giving the creature the maximum chance of survival. He desperately needed speech to allay any fears the new creature might have at finding him already on the planet, but so far he had not achieved much in that direction.

Bran left the cavern with a spring in his step, and looked around at what he now considered to be his world. Opening his mouth as wide as it would go, he let out a mighty roar of triumph, and the sound crashed back from the ice cliffs in a series of ringing echoes, a few loose fragments of ice tinkling down from the high ice shelf above.

There was a steady wind blowing and the clouds were thickening above, while a thin spattering of ice crystals lay on the stony ground, but not as yet enough to make travelling any easier. It was time to see if his food pods had dried out, and if they were, replace them with the next batch.

As he made his way to the fire chasm, he travelled some distance away from the ice cliff overhang, just in case some more of it came crashing down. He had a new awareness of himself, and was even more careful to make sure he didn't sustain any injuries through carelessness.

The crystal cave seemed even brighter somehow, and he felt compelled to enter. As he neared the centre, the light appeared to pulse slightly, and a faint high pitched sound tickled the hair in his ears. Again that odd feeling of being somewhere else overcame him, and then it was gone.

Something was in communication with him, and he wished he knew what, and was able to answer back. The feeling faded away, and the cave returned to normal.

Passing the bone cave, he noticed its barrier of bones were in place, and felt relieved as nothing had tried to escape into his world and cause problems. In the fire chasm the pods had dried, shrinking a little in the process, and were replaced with a new batch. He bit into one of the dried pods and was pleasantly surprised to find it was more enjoyable than when eaten raw. On the way out, he would harvested another load of hair, no longer feeling guilty for doing so as it grew back so readily and was only a plant, or was it?

The bone cave intrigued him. Why no skulls, where had they gone? They must surely have existed, all creatures had a head. And the very shape of the bones,why a sharp point on one end of some of them? Nature never brought something about without good reason, but he could see no reason for the points.

It was too much, he had to go in again. Carefully removing the bone barricade so that it could be put back together at speed, he squeezed into enigmatic cave.

The bones rattled and clanked as he moved about, alerting anything else which might be in the vicinity. Bran found some bones even bigger than any of his, and he tried to visualise how big the creature had been, and shuddered.

He sorted out a few bones he thought might come in useful, stacked them near the exit, and armed with along spear like bone, went into the next cave.

This one had the ubiquitous glowing moss, but of a slightly different colour, being a pale green blue. There was something about the light which hurt his eyes, and he passed through it quickly to the next one.

He left large footprints in the soft sandy floor of the caves, so he could easily find his way back to the exit in a hurry if need be. What surprised him was the lack of other footprints, the sand only had very indistinct marks, more like ripples, than marks of other creatures. But surely there must be some because of the bones?

Two caves on he saw the first sign of life. In the middle of the cave lay what looked like a large dark green beetle, its legs tucked up under its carapace. It looked lifeless somehow, was nearly three metres long and must have weighed about one hundred and fifty kilos in life. Bran approached it cautiously, and gave the casing a prod with the long bone, ready to beat a hasty retreat if it moved.

The prod produced a hollow ringing sound, and upon inspection the carapace was empty, even the legs had been cleaned out leaving only the hard hollow shell.

What kind of creature could do that? Was his first thought, and then he wondered if maybe it had died of old age, and lots of little things had cleaned out the shell. He still didn't want to meet them, large or small.

Bran suddenly had the feeling that something was watching him, and remembering the creature in the cave on the lower level where the floor had collapsed, beat a hasty retreat to the exit, and put the barrier bones firmly back in place.

Adding as many as he could of the bones he had selected into the carry bag, he made his way out of the tunnel system, stuffing the large bundle of hair into what little room remained in the bag, so most of it hung out and tickled his nose.

Once out in the open air he felt better, and noticed what looked like another storm brewing up. Dark scudding clouds hovered over the edge of the distant lower ice sheet, while a thin keening wind sighed as it raced up over the cliffs carrying a faint haze of ice crystals.

Back in the cavern, he tidily stacked the contents of the carry bag into their respective places, dropped a crystal into the box, let the disgorged capsule lie on the ice slowly decomposing, and had a meal.

Although his speech practice hadn't produced many easily

discernable words, he continued with it until his throat felt sore, gaining a few more words, and then fell asleep.

The dreams came and went as usual, but one persisted long after he had awakened. It concerned the large purple crystal he had found so long ago, and he felt he should do something with it, but what?

In the dream he seemed to be holding it and something wonderful happened, but he couldn't quite make out what it was.

Going over to the crystal pile, He lifted the huge crystal up and gazed at its beauty. A tiny light within the matrix danced about like a firefly and he was held spellbound for a few moments. Bran, not knowing what else to do, sat down, and cradled the crystal in his hands.

A faint sound, only just audible, seemed to fill the space around him, and as he relaxed the crystal seemed to get bigger, and then he and the crystal were one. He was somewhere out in space, speeding among the stars.

It wasn't frightening or unnerving in any way, suns blazed in all their glory and galaxies flashed by at enormous speed, and then he was confronted by a giant of a crystal, filling the heavens.

It seemed to be telling him something, and he understood it, but later he couldn't recall what it was, except that it had happened. And then he was back in the cavern, the light still danced within the crystal, and then that too faded from sight.

The crystal was just a crystal again, a thing of great beauty, but that was all. Bran had a strange feeling that everything was going to be alright, he need have no fear of the future now. He tried to recall what had happened, but the pictures faded as he looked at them, all he knew was that he was a part, albeit a very small part, of something greater and gained some sort of comfort from that.

It was almost like an anticlimax, nothing seemed important any more, and then he remembered the tasks which lay ahead. The timing of sending the crystals up to the Orbiter had to be just right, and he must have enough vocabulary to communicate convincingly to the new arrival, or everything he had been through would have been for nothing.

After something to eat, he felt better. The ice would return, life would be that little bit easier, and he had company coming soon.

With a renewed sense of purpose, Bran added sides to the sledge so that several carry bags could be transported without having to tie them down, he felt this was important, but was not quite sure why.

If he was to travel outside the ice region to find the green valley of his dreams, he would have to carry water with him in case there were places where there was none. He had no means of making a water proof container, but he could carry ice if he could insulate a bag sufficiently.

After his next rest period, he wove two bags, one slightly smaller than the other, and filled the gap between with fluffed up hair. He thought if he filled the bag with ice and left it near the edge of the fire chasm for a while, it would prove things one way or another.

Bran set off to try the test, noticing that the wind had gained in strength since he had been outside last, and ice flurries were billowing in sparkling clouds along the edge of the lower ice sheet.

He hurried down the tunnel to the fire chasm, leaving the bag full of ice as near the edge as he dared. On the way back he intended to gather more hair, but first he would take another look at the bone cave, and what lay beyond.

This time he took the red marker pod as foot prints were ephemeral in the soft sand of the caves, and there just might be something else in there which could obliterate them.

The bone barrier was removed and laid to one side and Bran entered the bone cave. He quickly made his way across the hard clanking bones as carefully as possible and into the next cave, leaving a red mark on the side wall where the two caves met.

Marking his way, he passed the beetle cave and into one which was a bit different. The roof of the cave seemed to be peppered with small holes and the floor beneath was fine sand without a mark on it. No foot prints? That was unusual, as all caves showed some movement of the sand.

Bran went back to retrieve the beetle carapace, pushing it with a long bone, he still didn't fancy actually touching it. He was surprised how easily it moved, and on close inspection found the actual shell was wafer thin.

Pushing it close to the area of unmarked sand, he gave it a kick, which sent it sliding across to the middle. As it came to rest, it rocked to and fro for a moment as if the creature was still inside.

A slight swishing sound made him look up as hundreds of thin grey tendrils slithered out of their holes down to encompass the carapace which disappeared from sight in the swirling mass. The tendrils continued to writhe about for a while, and then slowly withdrew to their respective holes in the roof of the cave.

The centre of the cave floor was now stained with a faint green colour, the pulverised remains of the beetle's outer casing. Bran felt a sense of shock, it would have been so easy to have walked across that cave, and he would have been no more.

Still shaking a little from the revelation of just how dangerous the caves could be, he returned to the exit cave, collected a few useful looking bones, put the barrier firmly back in place, and returned to his more predictable world outside the mountain caves.

The ice bag, he decided, would be left at the fire chasm for one rest period, and if it still contained some ice, then he would have a means of carrying a water supply when he went looking for the valley in his dreams.

After the usual meal and rest, Bran still couldn't get the picture of the cave with the all devouring tendrils out of his mind. What other horrors did the mountain contain? He began to wonder if it was wise to go there again, but he would have to retrieve the ice bag, if only to see if it had worked.

He couldn't remember how full the crystal collecting box was, but thought it about time he gave the others something to think about. Finding a small bone with a very sharp point, he pressed it into his arm to release a drop of blood which was then smeared onto a crystal, and as he put the crystal into the box he felt a sense of satisfaction at the thought he may cause a little concern to those who had incarcerated him on this world.

A massive thump resounded around the cavern and the ground shook. Bran hurried out to see what had happened.

In the far distance, well past the black rock, a cloud of ice crystals were begriming to settle. Something very large had come down from the upper sheet, and he though he had better go see what it was.

Although the ice storms, such as they were, had deposited some ice on the bare ground, it was not enough to make the going as easy as he was used to.

Reaching the fall site, it was plain to see what had caused the almighty thump. A block of ice, nearly as big as his cavern, had come away from the cliff.

Embedded in the clear blue ice he could see a huge construction, and it was big, much bigger then the carrier he had seen with corpse in it. This thing seemed different, apart from its size. It was cigar like in shape with bulbous attachments around what he thought was the middle. The metal hadn't corroded as had his first find, but the ice was too thick to even contemplate hacking his way in to it.

So it looks as if others have been down here, he thought. Perhaps they too were after the crystals, but gave up after their craft had crashed.

Looking around, Bran could see in the distance a column of water vapour rising up to meet the lowering clouds, and though it might be worth looking at as a possible heat source for drying his pods.

It turned out to be a hole in the ground surrounded by fallen ice from the cliffs above. The vapour was coming out in a series of puffs as if there was a restriction down there somewhere. He wondered just what would happen if he blocked it up with the fallen ice, and to satisfy his curiosity he set about piling up ice blocks around the hole in the form of an unstable wall.

When he thought it high enough, he gave the wall a good push, and with a satisfying rumble the whole thing fell into the hole. The water vapour gave a few pathetic puffs, and then gave up. That was a waste of effort, he said to himself, and began to slowly walk back towards his cavern.

Bran had only gone about three hundred metres when the ground shuddered and the hole spewed forth a mighty column of ice, rock, water vapour and anything else which had accumulated down there over time. Most of the detritus went straight up, and then fell down around the hole, but the sulphurous stench which followed it nearly made Bran bring up his last meal, and he resolved not to interfere with nature again, unless he really needed to.

Lightning began to flicker in the clouds over the lower ice sheet, the wind picked up carrying a few stinging particles of ice, and Bran thought it prudent to return to his cavern.

He was looking forward more than ever to the return of the colder conditions for which he had been constructed, ice was so much easier to travel over.

Bran had difficulty in judging the passing of time as there was no day and night as such. He slept and ate when he felt like it, but this was of little help. He wanted to gradually extend the period of time between each sending up of the box of crystals, so implying that things were getting difficult, but couldn't think of a way of doing so.

He went to sleep thinking about the problem, but was no wiser upon awakening. Time to check the pods, he thought, stretching his body and then consuming a quick meal.

Outside was looking promising as a thin layer of ice crystals had built up on the main track leading to the entrance to the mountain's core, and this made travelling so much easier.

The ice bag was still there, but a damp patch under the bag meant that some ice had melted. When Bran looked inside he was pleasantly surprised to find the bulk of the ice intact, and quite hard.

Pleased with his new creation, and resisting the temptation to venture into the bone cave and the horrors which lay beyond, he gathered another quantity of hair before leaving the tunnel system and straight out into a withering full blown ice storm.

The wind was howling up from the lower levels laden with ice crystals, and restricting his view to a few metres, not that he really minded as he was developing a sixth sense of where the track was, and only had to observe the upsweep of the crystal showers as they raced up over the cliffs to know he was on the right track.

On the way back to the cavern he made up his mind that the next time the collecting box was returned, he would leave it on the rock, indicating to those above that he had either run out of crystals, or had ceased to function. He just hoped he had got the timing right.

Speech practice went ahead interspersed with hair spinning and the weaving of bags to hold the dried pods, of which he now had a copious amount. Two more insulated ice bags were made ready for the long anticipated journey. As he put another crystal into the box, the lid snapped shut as did the dispensing slot, and he knew it was time to play dead.

The box was taken out and left on the black rock, never to be collected by him again. Somehow, he felt a cycle had been completed and was all the freer for realising it. This was now his world, he called the shots, and felt he could survive here very well.

One problem remained. How would he know when his replacement would arrive? He felt he needed to be there to greet her as she would be terrified from the experience and may do something detrimental to herself. All he could do was to keep a watch on the box, and if it was collected again he thought she would be sent down soon afterwards when they realised the crystal supply had ended.

His speech was improving bit by bit, new words being added along with a sore throat each time he forced his larynx to perform a duty it had not been designed for.

Bran decided to check the collecting box frequently after its return, and when it went up again empty, he would have to be ready to greet his replacement, and this meant an almost constant watch.

He had never slept outside his cavern, but didn't see any reason he shouldn't as there were no threats to his person that he knew of. It would be no colder than in his cavern, but the storm winds might hurl large blocks of ice around, and he didn't want to be hit by one. He reasoned the replacement would be set down somewhere near the cavern as she would need it to continue the collecting cycle. He only had to wait, and that he was not good at.

One sleep cycle later, and the box was back. Bran stared at it knowing he was irrevocably committed if he just left it there, but leave it there he did.

Not knowing what kind of terrain he was likely to travel over on his journey to the green valley, he strengthened the sledge, adding extra bones where he thought there might be a weakness, and adding extra bindings of hair and glue resin on the joints.

Food stocks were topped up, and a quantity of cords were made of different thicknesses to cope with all eventualities.

Every time he awoke from a rest period, he went out to the black rock to see if the collecting box was still there, and one 'day' it had gone. Now he would have to begin his vigil, spending each sleep period near the rock in case she was sent down. He managed to push a few blocks of fallen ice from the cliff overhang into a semicircle, providing a crude shelter from the prevailing winds, as the chill factor could be quite high in a storm.

As the ice storms increased in frequency, the temperature dropped, and the lower ice sheet crept ever closer to the cliffs. A good layer of crystals had built up and compacted, making travelling almost a pleasure, but the softice pools were getting less frequent. Although he had a good stock of dried food pods, he did begin to worry if they would be enough for the two of them if the softice pools disappeared altogether.

Fast asleep, tucked in behind his ice barrier, he was awoken by a deep throated rushing sound superimposed over the constant rushing noise of the wind. Shaking the accumulated ice crystals from his coat, he looked upwards but could only see the rushing clouds of ice crystals, but the sound was getting louder. And then a dark shape slowly emerged from the cloud base, and the noise hurt his ears.

A huge box-like construction surrounded in a cobweb of rods slowly lowered itself to the ice surface a mere fifty metres from the black rock.

As it settled down, the rods bent and buckled, absorbing the shock and what seemed to be a protective coating flaking off in a shower of fine particles. The rods began to crumble away as the corrosive atmosphere got to work, and soon just the box remained. Bran wondered what would happen next, remembering the last time he saw one of these containers locked in the ice. He cautiously approached the hulk, looking for the drop down door he had seen on the last one, but there was no sign of it.

Bran took a few paces back to see if he had missed anything, when without warning, one whole side of the box swung down to the ice with a crash which hurt his ears.

Looking inside he could just make out webbing holding a large bag-like structure, the surface of which seemed to move of its own accord. A rent in the surface appeared, followed by another, and then he could dimly make out the shape of a duplicate of himself.

Although he expected this, it was still a shock to see what looked like him hanging there in a web harness, and he wasn't sure what to do. At that moment there was a twang, and one of the straps broke, tilting his facsimile over to one side. Several more traps broke in quick succession, and she was free.

She stood there, looking dazed and frightened. Bran, not knowing what else to do, said 'Welcome, I am here to help you.' She shrank back, a look of pure horror on her face.

Bran stepped back a few paces, and beckoned her forwards.

A loud clang as something within the container succumbed to the atmosphere and fell, goading her towards the exit, and then she stepped out onto the ice.

Bran knew he had to be careful, and spoke only just loud enough to be heard over the constant howling wind.

'Follow me to the cavern, we can talk there.' his throat was already feeling the strain of forcing his larynx into shapes it was never intended for.

Slowly he backed away, and when there was some five metres between them, she hesitatingly followed. He went up the tunnel, and turned around to see she had stopped at the entrance.

Not knowing what else to do, Bran turned and went up to the far side of the cavern and sat down, thinking this was the least threatening posture to adopt. Slowly she came in and stood in the centre of the ice cave, still trembling a little, and looking furtively around.

'I expect they said you would be alone down here,' she nodded, and then seemed to relax a little. 'They sent you because they thought I had died. I fooled them into thinking I had. Two of us can survive here much better than one. There is nothing to be afraid of, you are welcome to share my home.'

Bran waited to see if she would speak, and then realised she would have to train her voice before they could communicate properly. 'You will not be able to speak until you have learned how to. I had to learn, and I will help you.' She uttered a deep growl as if trying to respond, and gave up.

'First you must eat,' and Bran slowly went over to the pile of pods under their protective cover of ice and picked up several pods of the two edible types, and offered them to her. She took them from him, and hesitatingly nibbled the end of one.

Bran heaved a sigh of relief, he had made contact, and now the slow process of acclimatizing her to this new world could begin.

Three:
Company

WHEN HIS NEW companion looked a little more settled, Bran tried to explain the system of the crystals, the collecting box and where he, and now she, fitted in. The collecting box brought the dawn of recognition to her eyes, and he then knew she had been programmed to do the same job as he had.

This meant she would only expect to eat the pods without the necessary minerals in them, so that the head pains would drive her to collect crystals. He explained this with his limited vocabulary, and she seemed to understand.

Getting across his aim to travel out to the green valley was a little more difficult, but he thought she got the gist of it.

They soon got into the rhythm of things, she seeming very keen to vocalise, and much to Bran's surprise, she learnt a lot quicker than he had.

By the time they had a useful vocabulary between them, Bran explained how they would delay the sending of the crystal box to simulate a difficulty in finding crystals, so preparing the time for their leaving the ice world and the long journey to the green valley.

He wasn't sure if she could be called back to the space station, and then remembered the unpleasant capsule he had taken just before going back himself. Perhaps if she didn't take one they couldn't call her back? He didn't know, but it seemed likely somehow. That capsule was part of the system, and if it was missing....? a chance they would have to take when the time came.

Several times he had asked her what her name was, but she was only able to make noises unlike any word he knew, but at last she managed it. 'Mali', and for the first time she beamed with delight. Bran had difficulty pronouncing it, but practising it when out of earshot helped until he was sound perfect. The bond between them grew, and Bran began to wonder how he could have stayed sane without her.

Bran explained about the large purple crystal, and the strange sensations he had when holding it. It wasn't until he had shown her the crystal cave, along with the others, that she made the suggestion that they take the crystal with them next time. He couldn't see why, but out of politeness, didn't argue.

Mali was not only free from the head pains due to the pod with the missing minerals being eaten, but she didn't seem to suffer from looking back into her past memory either.

Bran tried to explain what happened to him, long ago, and how he overcame the problem. He thought perhaps they had rushed things a little too much, and the mind block failed to work.

An ice storm of huge proportions thundered up against the cliffs, sending blasts of ice crystals into the cavern and making their ears pop with the concussion wave as it raced up the tunnel. The lightning was as bad as he had ever known it, and trying not to show his fear, failed miserably.

After the storm had subsided to a more reasonable level, they both curled up together and slept deeply. When they awoke, a new layer of ice had been deposited all along the old track way under the cliffs, the softice pools had disappeared altogether and there was no sign of the red crystal bearing rock.

Bran thought it time they left the area, as without food pods their supplies would run out after a while, but first a few more crystal deliveries must be made.

When they next went to the tunnels under the mountain, Mali insisted they bring the large crystal. After a fair bit of mumbling under his breath about the irrationality of the female sex, Bran complied. They entered the tunnel and hurried along to the crystal cave. 'I think you're meant to take it in.' said Mali, with a knowing smile.

Bran gave her a doubtful look, but walked to the centre. The myriad crystals in the wall of the cave seemed to glow extra bright, and a high pitched tone rang in the air. Bran wanted to leave, but was rooted to the spot.

The crystal in his hands seemed almost alive as the light got even brighter, and the sound was now so loud it hurt his ears.

He wanted to drop the crystal and clap his hands over his ears. He tried, but couldn't move.

There was sudden surge of energy, and space itself seemed to warp. And then all was quiet, all the crystals had gone leaving just the holes in the wall where they had been. In his hand was a small deep purple crystal with a tiny pin point of light racing around inside it.

Bran staggered out of the cave, his legs barely able to hold him up. Mali still had that smile on her face as he approached, 'You knew that would happen, didn't you?'

'I knew something would happen' she replied, 'but wasn't sure what.'

'I could have been killed in there', he said reproachfully.

'No, I wouldn't have let you go in there if I thought that would happen. Somehow I knew the big crystal needed to be in that cave for something very important to happen, and it has, thanks to you.'

He showed her the little crystal in his hand, the tiny pin point of light only just visible now, but still dancing around.

'I think it's a present for what you did', she said, excitedly.

'It's a what?' Bran exclaimed, 'They were only crystals, just minerals, stuck in the cave wall'.

'I think there's a little more to it than that', she replied patiently, 'There's something well beyond our understanding going on, we are only a tiny but important part of it. One day we'll know, I feel sure of that'. He felt like arguing, but knew better, she was usually right.

They left the cave complex, Bran a little more contrite as the full significance of what had happened dawned upon him. They were to talk about the cave and its crystals many times in the future, it was a wondrous thing, and barely within their range of comprehension.

On the way back to the cavern, Bran explained why he thought they should leave soon, as there were no signs of the softice pools, and without them their food supplies would dwindle to nothing. Mali suggested they had a good look first, which they did, but the further down the lower ice sheet they went, the harder the ice became.

'How did you manage before?' She asked.

'There were always softice pools, as far as I can remember,' Bran replied, 'but I've never known it to be so cold before.' She asked where they would go to find the green valley, and Bran explained how he had seen it in his dreams, and once up on the upper ice sheet, he had seen the mountains of his dreams on the horizon.

'We'll have to pull the sledge with our supplies up onto the upper ice sheet, and head off towards the mountains, I only hope our food supplies will last.' He explained about the ice bags which would supply them with water when they left the frozen areas, but Mali looked a little doubtful.

They had just left the crystal box out for collection, when Mali stopped in her tracks, Bran bumping into her ample rear end as he had his head down to keep the ice crystals out of his eyes. She turned, and gave him one of those knowing looks only a female can. He would have blushed if it hadn't been so cold.

'Does the wind always blow up over the cliffs in the same direction?' she asked. He replied that it did, as far as he knew. 'So it must carry on towards the mountains then, in the same direction that we must go?'

Bran shrugged his shoulders, wondering what was coming next. 'If that is so,' she carried on, 'we could weave a sheet of material, attach some cords, and let the wind pull us along.' Bran was dumb struck for a moment, this was clear logical thinking, and he wished he'd thought of it first.

Later, they set to and wove the sail, adding extra runners at the rear end of the sledge so that they could ride on it if the wind was strong enough. Bags of dried pods, insulated bags of ice chips, and a selection of useful looking bones were loaded onto the sledge in readiness for their journey.

They took it outside for a trial run, and although it was hard work, they managed to pull it along, Bran in a harness at the front, and Mali pushing from behind. She had platted a belt with a small pouch on it to carry the purple crystal, explaining that she felt it must be carried with them at all times,

'I'm sure it's for our protection.' she insisted. Bran just nodded, saying nothing.

The day came for the final crystal delivery, and Bran thought they wouldn't fill the box, as it would give the impression that the crystal supply had dried up. They left it on the black rock, took one last look around the cavern which had been their home for so long, and set off along the ice cliff towards the long slope down which Bran had slid so long ago.

An extra steep section halfway up made them stop for a rest. 'If we slip now, the whole damn thing will just shoot down to the bottom, I think we ought to drive a long bone into the ice, attach a strong cord and move the sledge up bit by bit. If we slip, the cord should hold it.'

It took longer than they expected, and by the time they had reached the top they were exhausted. The ice sheet stretched out before them in a long continuous gentle slope towards the distant dark blue mountain range.

After a short rest Mali unfolded the sail, attached the holding cords and threw the sail up into the air. It billowed out like a living thing as the wind caught it, jerking the sledge forward.

With Mali riding on the extended runners and Bran adding a push when the wind strength lessened, they were under way towards their goal. The sledge sped along, the runners singing on the hard ice, and at times they were both able to enjoy a ride on the sledge as the wind increased on the higher slopes.

Several times they dropped the sail for a rest break and food, noticing the ridge they had climbed to get onto the upper ice sheet had now disappeared in a haze, and the smudge on the horizon was taking on a more solid form as they drew closer to the Blue Mountains.

At long last and feeling exhausted, they reached the top of the ridge. Below them lay another huge sheet of ice which terminated in a bank of mist, so what lay there was a mystery, but the mountains could now be seen quite clearly.

'Well, that's the worst part over.' said Mali, heaving a sigh of relief.

'Wouldn't bet on that,' Bran replied, 'this planet is full of surprises, I'm forever being caught out.'

The sail was put away and Bran thought a breaking system was needed for the sledge, as it was difficult to judge the steepness of the slope in the distance, and once out of control, there would be nothing they could do to stop it.

Jamming a long bone between the runners seemed a good idea, and they tried it on the first part of the slope, bringing the sledge to halt in a shower of ice chips.

The long journey down the ice slope began, Bran pressing down hard on the long bone when he thought the speed was excessive, while Mali seemed to be enjoying the thrill of it and constantly called for more speed.

As the bottom of the slope neared, the ice turned softer and built up against the runners causing them to stop once in a while to free off the impacted slush. Bran, having experienced pulling the sledge over hard ground was not looking forward to the end of the ice, and said so.

'There are two of us now, we should be able to manage it.' Mali, ever the optimist, replied. Bran was not too convinced.

The slush ice gave way to fine gravel to be later replaced with rounded pebbles, the runners of the sledge squealing as they dragged it along. It was hot work, and they stopped frequently to refresh themselves with ice chips. 'Hope we find water soon,' said Bran, 'this ice isn't going to last for ever.' Mali just smiled and nodded.

Bran was also concerned about the wear on the runners. They had a few spare bones, but not the long ones used for the runners, and there was no more glue to lock them in place anyway.

In the distance the stones gave way to a more rocky terrain, and Bran's heart sank. There was no way they could drag the heavy sledge over rocks. As they reached the first of a series of rocky ridges, it was decided to take a rest, and try to work out what to do next.

Bran had picked up a pretty stone. It was egg-shaped and felt very heavy for its size. As he turned it over in his hand his peripheral vision clouded, and all he could see was the coloured banding on the stone. Mali stepped forward, and with a sharp chop to his wrist the stone flew from his grasp.

'What the hell did you do that for?' asked an astonished Bran. 'Take a look at the stone.' Mali replied. Ten needle sharp claws were slowly retracting back into the body of the stone to leave no trace of their existence. 'If that thing got a grip on your hand, how do you think you would get it off?'

Bran reluctantly apologised for his outburst.

Mali wandered off to see what lay ahead, and came back with good news. 'There's a smooth sandy track just up ahead, and it seems to run up to the start of the rock cliffs.'

They got into the double harness with renewed hope, maybe there was a way through. 'This track is the same width all along,' Bran observed, 'and that's not natural. Something must have made it.' he added as an after thought.

Some two hundred metres on they came to a large hole in the mountain side, and the soft sandy track went into it.

'Maybe there is a way through.' said Mali. They pulled the sledge over to a gap in the rocks, and Bran cautiously entered the cave. Mali was just about to follow when Bran came running out at high speed. 'There's something coming,' he yelled 'get up into the rocks and get ready to throw one if it seems aggressive.' They had barely reached the sanctuary of the rocks when out of the cave there came another of the planet's strange life forms.

Ovaloid in shape and twice as long as them both put together, it looked like half a grey melon slowly moving along the track. They could see no head or eyes to guide it, but it seemed to know where it was going. As it went by, Bran reached out and gave it a kick. It took no notice of this affront to its person, and Bran got a sore foot for his trouble. 'It felt like solid stone.' he exclaimed. As it slowly progressed up the path, seemingly unaware of the two strangers in it's midst, Mali suggested they follow it to see what it did.

The creature reached the point where they had entered the track, and there it stopped, or seemed to. It was now moving very slowly, and a grinding noise could be heard. As it inched forward, a new layer of sand trailed out behind it.

'It's eating rock!' Bran declared, 'and shoving it out the back in the form of sand.'

The Stone Cropper very slowly crept forward, grinding away at the stones which lay in its path, totally oblivious to the pair of interlopers in its territory. 'If you look carefully at the stones,' said Mali, 'you'll see little lines of something on them, I'll bet they are organic and possibly go right through the stone, break one open and have a look.' she said to Bran.

He picked up a stone, examined it, and brought it crashing down on a nearby rock. 'You're right, there's a fine filigree of something going right through it. The creature must extract it and use it for food. I'd love to see its teeth, they must be quite something.' 'Probably made of quartz, or something like it.' offered Mali.

They left the Stone Cropper to its meal and returned to the cave opening with the sledge. 'There's just a chance it might go right through,' said Mali 'I don't think the Cropper would need a shelter, it looks indestructible.'

They left the sledge at the entrance and walked in until it got too dark to see any real detail. As their eyes got used to the gloom, it was apparent that the walls of the tunnel had something on them similar to the moss in the caves back in Bran's old world, although not so bright.

Mali stooped to pick up some sand from the tunnel floor, and holding her hand up high, left it trickle out. 'Look, the finer particles drift down the tunnel, that means there is an air draft, and it must go out somewhere.' Bran looked apprehensive.

The alternative to the tunnel seemed insurmountable, as the mountain chain went on for as far as they could see in both directions, the towering cliff walls far too steep for them to climb. They returned to the sledge for food and water, only to find the remaining ice bag had only a few chips left, the rest having melted and soaked into the material.

They ate some pods, washed down with the remaining ice chips, Bran insisting that Mali had the ice while he squeezed the bag for his share. 'Not many pods left either.' Bran added gloomily.

It was decided to try the tunnel, the faint air flow giving them a little hope in an otherwise hopeless situation. As their supplies had been reduced to a bag of pods, cord, and a few bones, the sledge was left behind, Mali carrying the food while Bran put the cord and bones into another bag, and hung it around his neck.

Once their eyes had got accustomed to the gloom, they were able to proceed at a fair pace through the rift in the mountain.

'Looks as if the mountain has split, and the Cropper has eaten all the loose rocks on the ground.' said Bran, wanting to hear something apart from the soft padding of their feet

He could see Mali was flagging as she had dropped some way behind him, so he called a halt. The tunnel at this point had opened out into a large cavern, the roof being out of sight. 'Can you hear that?' asked Mali, after they had sat down at the side of the tunnel, 'sounds like the drip of water.' They searched but found nothing as the echo effect in the cavern disguised the source of the sound.

Mali had sat down again when Bran called out excitedly 'Look at this, seems like a damp patch on this rock.' A section of the tunnel wall was indeed damp, almost wet, and faintly glistening. Bran touched a finger to it and put it in his mouth. 'Tastes alright, a bit metallic though.'

Bran dug into his carry bag and produced a sharp pointed bone, and picking up a small rock the Cropper had missed, proceeded to chip away at the wet rock. He was on the point of giving up when a thin spurt of water shot out across the tunnel.

They dank their fill of the ice cold water when the was a sharp crack, and a piece of rock flew across the tunnel. They both jumped back as a torrent of water gushed out of the enlarged hole, hitting the far wall and quickly formed a pool on the tunnel floor.

'There's one hell of a pressure behind that,' Bran exclaimed, 'I think we'd better get out of here.' They both took off at a fast trot, the sound of the rushing water adding to the pounding of their feet.

Another sharp crack followed by a heavy thump was joined by a deep rushing sound, as the mountain's water cistern began to empty into the tunnel. They both broke into a fast gallop simultaneously as the roar of the water turned into a deep thunderous rumble.

Bran looked over his shoulder to see a foaming wave of water gaining on them, and called for more speed. The floor of the tunnel began to slope upwards, and their pace slowed accordingly. 'Come on Mali,' Bran gasped, 'it looks like a light ahead.'

They both pounded on towards the exit, and shot out into the blazing light of day. 'Cover your eyes.' Bran called out, blindly wheeling around to the left as the roar of the water caught up with them. They both scrambled up a mound of gravel next to the exit as the torrent of water burst out of the mountain and roared down the slope.

At the bottom of the slope, a line of rocks formed a ridge and a lake of water soon formed, deepening as they watched in astonishment.

'I can't believe the amount of water that's coming out, where do you think it's coming from?' asked Mali. Bran told her about the melt water he had seen back in his ice world. 'It must be the same here, collecting in the fissures deep within the mountain, over a long time.'

They sat there, high up on the gravel ridge getting their breath back, and watching the waters rise ever higher. At last the water cistern exhausted itself, only a trickle now issuing from the tunnel, while below them was a shimming blue lake.

'How about a swim?' suggested Mali. Removing their carry bags they both plunged into the lake, Bran powering out towards the middle to show his prowess and strength, but not quite knowing why. Nature, in its own inimitable way was setting things up for the future, as Bran would find out later.

'I had no idea we were so grubby,' exclaimed Mali, shaking the excess water from her now gleaming silver white coat, adding 'I hardly recognised you.' as she turned to run off. Bran managed to give her a good hard slap on the rump before giving chase to his companion. After they had dried off in the warm air, Bran suggested they pick up the carry bags and resume their journey before the food ran out completely.

Ahead lay another smaller mountain range, far too steep to climb, so a way through was sought. A deep rift in the rock mass looked promising, and they began the long climb up.

Nearing the top, the rift opened out to a flat area, on the side of which a trickle of water was falling from an overhang above. 'Do you think it's drinkable?' asked Mali. Bran cupped his hands and took a sip. 'Seems good to me, quite sweet in fact.' he replied. They quenched their not inconsiderable thirst, and sat down to rest.

Looking around, Bran spotted something unusual. 'That looks like a plant to me, the first we've seen since our pod plants,' he said, going over to one side of the rift to a pile of damp stones. On a small ledge, a grey leafed growth, a metre high, had established itself.

Upon close inspection they could see a myriad of small insect like creatures crawling about, nibbling the edges of the leaves. What looked like a brown stone just below the plant, slowly moved out a little, and a thin whip like tongue lashed upwards to pick off one of the insects, and then retracted into its mouth.

'If the plant gets its nutrient from the rock and water, the insects from the plant and the stone thing from the insects, what eats the stone thing?' asked Bran.

Mali shrugged her shoulders, and said 'I hope it's not too big, or we could have a problem.' They both stood there fascinated by the endless cycle of life before them, until they heard a distinctly metallic clanking noise somewhere above them.

'Get back under this overhang,' said Bran quietly, recognising the sound of a mechanical construction. 'I think we have a visitor.'

High above in a cleft between the rocks they could just make out the shiny outline of an ovaloid shape with rotary track drivers beneath it.

'Do you think they've sent something to spy on us?' asked Mali, looking worried for the first time.

'Doubt that,' replied Bran 'it's probably one of the devices they use to look for crystals, but we mustn't let it see us, or there could be trouble. It's looking lens is pointing down the rift so we had better go up a little, that way it'll have it's back to us. I wonder why it hasn't corroded, all the ones back at the ice cavern did in a very short time. They must have got some new protective coating, 'cos that one looks like new.'

The searcher robot gave a sudden lurch, and fell into a convenient gap. The traction engine whined and then burnt itself out, finally locking the robot irrevocably into the rocks until mother nature reduced it back to it's component parts.

Leaving the searcher robot to gaze down into the ravine, they climbed higher up the rift, pausing once in a while to get their breath back and looking down on what they had left. The lake was still there, shimmering in the weak sunlight, while they could just make out the odd shape of the Stone Cropper as it left the tunnel at great speed, and plunged into the lake. They didn't see it again until it emerged at the far end of the lake to disappear behind some rocks.

'Good thing we weren't in the tunnel when it went through,' commented Bran, 'or we'd have been crushed flat, and just look at the speed it was going, we couldn't have outrun it anyway.' They continued on up the rift, until it opened out a little, and there was their next barrier. Facing them was a huge blue and pale green wall of ice towering some ten metres above them, blocking the rift completely.

As they drew nearer, they could see what had caused it. A steam vent near one side of the rift was billowing clouds of water vapour, and the wind was blowing it due south towards the ice wall where it was adding to the already thick block of ice.

There seemed no way through or past it, because of its height and thickness. Bran swore quietly under his breath, but Mali got the message. They stood there studying it for what seemed like an eternity. Finally Mali said 'Remember the hole you told me about, the one which you blocked up, and it almost exploded after a while?' Bran nodded as he recalled the incident. 'Well, look up just above the vent, see that ledge sticking out? If you could make it more active, it would then go sideways, and maybe melt the ice.'

Bran went up to the vent for a closer look. There was enough loose rock lying around to do what he had done before, but the vent wasn't very active.

'Well, we've nothing to lose, may as well give it a go.' he commented. They set to collecting all the loose rock in the area, building a wall around the vent which was only just stable enough to hold itself together.

When they had run out of rocks, Bran stood back to survey their work. 'Stand well back Mali, if it works, stuff could fly anywhere, and remember these are rocks, not ice.' With that he gave the wall a push and it fell apart, most of it going down the vent hole.

Bran backed away from the hole to what he thought was a safe distance, and waited. The gentle stream of water vapour had ceased, even the feeble hiss which had accompanied it, and all was silent, except for the distant drone of the wind as it slipped over the top of the rocks above them

Bran joined Mali some way down the rift, his patience slowly evaporating as the minutes drifted by. 'It doesn't look like.......' A deep rumble could be felt beneath their feet, the mountains seemed to shudder, and then the vent reopened with a vengeance.

A blast of steam and water vapour hit the ledge and diverted across towards the ice wall, and the ice began to melt. 'Well thought out Mali, you should have been an engineer.'

'How do you know I wasn't? She replied with one of her challenging smiles, she liked to keep her man on his toes. As they watched the steam cutting into the ice, they ate half the remaining pods, which didn't amount to very much, and drank copiously from the warm melt water which was now running clear. 'How long do you think it will take?' she asked, mainly for something to say. 'Don't know how thick it is.' Bran replied glumly.

Sitting there, huddled together on a ledge just above the now rushing melt water, they waited to see if their plan would work before they starved to death

Bran had dozed off and awoke with a start as Mali gave him a dig in the ribs. 'Think it's working,' she said, 'there's a small hole in the ice, I can just see the sky through it.'

Both went as near as they dared to the roaring steam vent, and sure enough there was hole, and it was getting bigger as they watched. By the time the hole was big enough for them to have got through, the steam was just blasting though the middle, and no more ice was melting.

'Now what do we do, we'll be cooked alive if we try to get though that.' Mali waited patiently for Bran to work it out, rather than tell him what she thought was obvious.

After much thought, Bran said 'If we could remove that ledge just above the vent, the stream would go straight up, and we could then get through.' Mali smiled to herself. The hunt for a suitable sized rock took them some time, and a long journey down the rift, but find one they did. Bran pushed it towards the edge of the vent with the longest bone he had, and stepped smarty back.

The steam column hesitated for a moment, and then the rock came hurtling out, hitting the ledge fair and square.

A large piece flew off to one side, and the steam column bent away from the ice wall, leaving the hole clear.

Their combined sigh of relief could almost be heard over the hiss of the steam. Bran went up to the hole and called back to Mali 'We can get through alright, but I can't see what's on the other side. You had better hold my back legs while I crawl in.'

Bran had already heaved himself up onto the edge of the hole and moved slowly forward, Mali rushed up to grab his rear legs in case he slipped through into the unknown.

The hole in the ice wall was some ten metres deep, and a tight fit for both of them. Bran's head poked out of the hole and he then froze.

'I'm coming back.' he called out, and they both shuffled back out of the hole.

When they had got their breath back, Bran explained why he had retreated, and what he had seen.

'There's a drop of some two metres on the other side, down to a very steep ice slope for some way. It gets less steep further down and then it's all misty, so I can't see what's there. It's far too steep to just slide down, we'd be going at one hell of a lick if we tried, and we don't know what's at the end of the slope. You have a look and see what you think.'

Mali was surprised she'd been asked for her opinion, but obliged. 'If we hammer some bones into the ice and lower ourselves on a cord, we can get down to the slope. You once told me how you went down an ice slope using two bones to lessen your speed, do you think it would work here?' Bran thought for a moment, and said 'It's our only chance. Can't see any other way of getting down.'

With Mali holding his legs, Bran drove two pointed bones into the lip of the hole, attached a pair of the thickest cords they had, and carefully lowered himself down to the ice slope. Mali passed down two more bones, and they were anchored into the ice at the top of the slope so Bran had something to hold onto.

The carry bags were passed down, followed by a trembling Mali, as she attached herself to the other anchor bone.

'We'll have to go down backwards with a bone in each hand,' said Bran, stating the obvious, 'it should lessen our speed, I hope. Are you ready?' She nodded. With the carry bags around their necks, the pair let go of the anchor bones, and began their descent.

They seemed to almost fall, such was the velocity, ice chips streaming out behind them in a white flurry, accompanied by the scream of the protesting ice slope.

Mali looked terrified as they hurtled down the slope, wondering if they would stop before they hit something unyielding. Their arms burned with fire from the strain of ramming the bones into the hard ice, but as they drew nearer the bottom of the steep section, the ice was softer, and they slowed down considerably.

Eventually the pair came to a halt on the flatter part of the ice, but there was still some way to go before they reached the band of mist which obscured what lay beyond. Because their feet had been designed to work efficiently on flat ice, it was not difficult for them to carry on in a more dignified manner towards their goal, after a short rest and half the remaining pods had been eaten.

The ice turned into slush as they approached the long line of mist which shrouded the terrain. 'Better slow down a bit,' said Bran, 'there's no telling what lies ahead.' The swirling clouds of cooling whiteness were refreshing after their last experience, but could also hide unknown dangers.

They moved slowly forwards, and then realised they had lost all sense of direction. 'This sometimes happens when you can't see where you're going,' Bran announced, 'and you wind up going in circles. I'll go ahead until you can only just see me, then you come forward and do the same, it should work,' he added hopefully.

The mist thinned after what seemed like an eternity, and they were out in clear air. Before them stretched an area of shrubs and bushes, dotted about on a plain of gravel with a slight upwards slope, so they couldn't see what lay in the far distance.

They trudged on, looking for anything which looked remotely edible on the plants around them, but there were no pods or berries, just leaves, and they had a dull green unpleasant look about them, along a pungent smell.

'There are only a few pods left,' said Mali, 'so we may as well eat them, but water is going to be our main problem.' Bran just grunted, he was well aware of that.

At the top of the rise they stopped in awe. There before them was the promised land of Bran's dreams. They were on the edge of a high cliff overlooking what looked like paradise. Grassy mounds, little silver streams, bushes of every shape and size with various trees dotted about among them spread out to the faint haze of a mountain range on the horizon.

Bran went up to the edge of the cliff and looked down. 'I thought it was too easy,' he exclaimed, 'there's one hell of a drop to the ground below, and it's sheer all the way down. There's a lot of trees at the bottom, but it looks as if their branches die and fall off if they touch the cliff, 'cos there's a pile of them all along the bottom, and they're bleached white. They walked along the cliff top, looking for a way down, when there was a deep throated growl from behind one of the patches of scrub.

Bran immediately drew his club bone from the bag and faced the scrubby bushes from which the sound seemed to emanate. Another growl, and a nightmare on legs stepped out of the scrub. A body half the size of Bran's supported a mean looking head armed with a set of razor sharp teeth, which were on full display. A pair of almost black eyes surveyed the pair, flicking from one to the other.

The creature slowly edged forward until it was within range of Bran's club, who then swung it down hard on the snout barely two metres before him. A yelp of pain, and the creature backed into the shrubby at high speed. Bran advanced up to the shrubs, but there was no sign of the creature, as far as he could tell.

With Bran in the lead, they carried on along the cliff edge looking for a way down. A kilometre on and they found a series of faults in the cliff, forming ten metre high steps which led down to the plain below.

A rustle in the bushes and a deep growl indicated that their adversary had not forgotten the whack on the nose, and was game for more of the same.

Bran was right on the edge of the cliff, not a good position to be in as it left little room for manoeuvre. With a threatening snarl, the creature launched it's attack straight at Bran, who right at the last moment stepped to one side and clouted his attacker on the rear end as it tried to stop, but not before it had lashed out a clawed limb and just grazed Bran's arm.

Its forward momentum plus the whack from Bran toppled it over the edge. A series of howls and grunts signalled it's decent to the ground beneath, as it bounced from ledge to ledge.

'That was a near thing.' said Mali, looking worried at the thought of what might have happened. 'Didn't like doing that,' Bran replied, 'but I had little choice really. It was only defending its territory against something new to it.'

Surveying the ledges, it was decided to use the cords to abseil down one ledge at a time, using a rock as a belay point where possible, as the bone supply was running low.

On the last ledge they were in for a shock. 'I don't like the look of this,' Bran called out, leaning over the edge, 'what I thought was a tangle of dead branches is in fact a collection of bleached bones. There's hundreds of 'em, must be from animals who've fallen over the edge.'

At that moment there was rustle from above, and what they assumed to be their assailant's mate poked her nose over the edge of the cliff.

Either the edge gave way, or it leaned out too far and lost its balance while looking for its mate, but its fate was just the same as it came bouncing down the steps one after the another, narrowly missing Mali, to fall in a heap at the bottom.

What happened next shocked them both. The trees nearest the fallen creature bent down, embracing it in their branches until it was obscured from view. When the branches eventually returned to their normal position, another little pile of bones had been added to those already there.

'You could have been that animal if you'd gone down,' Mali said shaking, 'so now what do we do?' Bran looked lost in thought for a moment, 'It looks as if the trees are there to prevent anything from the upper plain getting down, and altering the balance of whatever life exists there. Can't think of any other reason, can you?' Mali shook her head.

They sat there, wondering how to overcome this new obstacle. 'There's nothing for it, I'll have to go down bit by bit on a cord, and see if I get the same reaction. If the trees start to bend over, yell, and help pull me back up.'

Mali did her best to dissuade him, but failed, his mind was made up. With tears in her brown eyes, Mali lowered the cord bit by bit as Bran sort new foot holds on his way down.

He stopped when level with the nearest tree, but it hadn't moved. He went down a little lower, and still no reaction from the guardian trees. Holding his breath, Bran finally stepped onto the pile of clanking bones at the bottom of the cliff, and still the trees didn't move. 'Give us a hand, Mali, I'm coming up again.'

With Bran safely back on the ledge, they were still no further in solving the problem. 'There's got to be a reason why the trees didn't react to me,' Bran said, 'there's just got to be, but what it?'

Hunger and thirst were now taking their toll, they desperately needed to get down to the land below, but the guardian trees firmly stood in their way.

'What makes my body different from other creatures on this world?' asked Bran.

'Nothing,' Mali replied, 'it's made from the same basic materials, so you said, so there must be something else we haven't thought of.'

A gentle breeze swept up from the valley below, warm, and slightly perfumed with the scent of the many flowering bushes and trees, adding to their frustration.

'I can only think of one thing which might make you different,' Mali said hesitatingly, 'and that's the crystal, nothing else has one.'

'Oh, come on, it's only a piece of mineral.' Bran replied crossly.

'I'm not so sure of that. There's nothing else I can think of,' Mali said patiently, 'you could go down carefully and when near a branch, take out the crystal and see if there's a reaction.'

The sight of the little streams meandering between the grassy knolls was too much in the end for Bran, who by now had a raging thirst.

'Ok, let me down slowly, I'll give it a try.' As he neared the first branch, he withdrew the crystal from its pouch, the tiny pinpoint of light was racing around excitedly within the purple matrix, and Bran held it out towards the branch.

First a few leaves twitched, he extended his arm and the branch itself moved out of the way. In disbelief, Bran stepped down onto the pile of bleached bones and waved his arm around. The trees came alive, swishing their branches out of the way of the glowing crystal, and he knew there was a safe passage through the barrier.

With Mali down beside him, Bran moved forward through the guardian trees, their branches obligingly swinging back from the pair, and they were out on the grassy lawn of the valley. Mali tied to not give Bran that 'I told you so' look, but he picked it up anyway and said 'That was a good bit of thinking, Mali, I wouldn't have thought of that.'

They hurried over to the nearest water, Bran cupping his hands and taking a sip. The look on his face said it all, and they both drank deeply.

'Now we need to eat.' Mali said, looking around at the various fruits and berries which adorned the nearby bushes.

'That could be tricky,' Bran replied, 'we don't know what's safe.' Mali looked down at the crystal pouch and then up at her companion.

The crystal was held next to a deep green globe like fruit, and the single pin point of light was joined by another adding a glow to the crystal.

'That one looks alright.' said Mali, plucking the fruit from its branch and taking a bite before Bran could stop her.

After a quick reprimand for taking unnecessary risks, they checked out the various fruiting bodies to be found on most plants. Very few proved negative, a notable exception being a grey shiny berry which shrivelled up upon contact with the crystal, so they would avoid anything like it in future.

Having eaten and drunk all they could to satiate their needs, they wandered along the stream with its crystal clear waters to a clearing among the trees in which stood a building. It seemed to be constructed from a series of hexagonal columns of white translucent marble, in the shape of a dome with one small entrance.

'That's something I didn't expect to see!' Bran exclaimed, 'looks like someone has been here before us.'

'I don't think so, somehow,' Mali replied, 'it's for us.'

Bran gave her one of those looks, but didn't dare say anything. The opening was only just big enough for them to squeeze in, but surprisingly there was plenty of room inside.

A pale soft light lit up the smooth inside of the dome, and Bran felt uneasy as they cast no shadows from its glow. Mali coyly snuggled up to him, 'It's nice in here, isn't it?'

Bran felt something he had not experienced for a long time, and then embarrassment, especially as he wasn't sure what it was.

After deciding to make the dome their base, they set off to explore their new territory.

High above them, circling the planet, the Orbiter was in a state of flux. They had called up the crystal collecting box.

The station commander was called when it was discovered the box only held a few crystals.

The survival tank was inspected, and found to be in perfect working order. 'Right, bring her back up.' ordered the commander. 'We can't,' one of the technicians replied nervously, 'she hasn't taken the last capsule in the box down there, and without it she won't go into a coma, so we can't call her back.' The commander went very pale and began to tremble. 'You've got to,' he squeaked, 'I command it.' The technician began to speak, thought better of it, and coughed instead.

The commander flounced out of the room and locked himself in his cabin for three days, after which they broke the door down and the chief medic was called. After four eye watering injections he became reasonably compos mentis, and was persuaded to signal Base about what had happened. Shortly afterwards, a new batch of materials arrived, claiming to be impervious to the planet's corrosive atmosphere. The machine shops fairly hummed, as did the operatives forced into treble shifts.

The new materials may well have been tougher, but they were also a lot harder to fabricate, and this just piled on the pressure.

The first batch of robot explorers were made ready and sent down. The first two landed a short distance apart and mistakenly thought the other was what they had been sent down to collect, so they just grappled each other to pieces in a vain attempt to make a capture.

Others did better, one actually getting into the cavern where it collected up some of Bran's bone stocks, and trundled out of the tunnel with them.

Unfortunately, a large blade bone obscured one of the vision eyes, and the robot plus bones dropped into a crevice in the ice sheet, where it thrashed away with its drive tracks digging ever deeper until its batteries ran out, and then lay motionless, still clutching the bones in a vice-like grip.

One explorer found the tunnel to the fire chasm, paused at the crystal cave sending back very clear pictures of where hundreds of crystals had been, which didn't exactly cheer anyone up very much.

It clattered its way on down the tunnel, startling the slimy thing in the cave of water and green drapes, and then slithered down the slope into the fire chasm cave.

The operator got a clear view of the cords Bran had left up for drying his pods but didn't see how close to the edge of the chasm the robot was. The tracks were sent into reverse just too late to stop the little robot from teetering over the edge, sending back amazing pictures of the molten lava bubbling away below, waiting to receive it.

The pictures of the drying cords were scrutinised in great depth and caused a lot of interest and speculation, giant spider's webs being the favourite, but no one realised the real purpose.

A rumour about a visit from some really high ranking VIP's, initiated by the sump cleaner's assistant, galvanised everyone into an even higher level of panic. As wages for the mission were extremely high, and everyone's credits were mounting up to unbelievable levels, no one wanted to be dismissed from this lucrative tour of duty, despite the hardships.

Two more robots were cobbled together from the remains of the new materials, one went to the hot zone and melted upon impact, while the other managed a little better.

Landing just above the fern-like plant with the mould growing on it, but jamming itself into a crevice as it did so, it therefore became immobile. Crystal clear pictures were sent back of the plant, the mould, the little insects which lived off the mould, and the stone like creature which licked the insects off the plant whenever it felt hungry.

A small group devoted themselves to the study of the stone like creature, even giving it a name. The whole thing was on the verge of developing a religious connotation when the atmosphere finally got to the transmitter. The picture degraded, changed colour at random, inverted, distorted, and eventually faded out altogether. It was a pity really, as they had got quite attached to the insect eating stony thing.

When it was realised the rumoured VIPs weren't coming, things got back to a near state of normality.

When the real VIP's arrived a few days later, all hell broke loose. Half the crew were sent back to base for counselling, being replaced by a bunch of tough, square jawed individuals who were really going to make things tick. After several days, the only thing ticking was the head cook's watch.

He like old fashioned things, and had spent a small fortune on it several years ago, but it didn't keep very good time because of the heat and grease it was exposed to.

As yet, no one had seen a crystal, let alone retrieved one.

There was loose talk of the station shutting down, which caused even more panic when they realised it would be the end of a very lucrative mission.

Two of the 'square jaws' offered to go down to the planet, but changed their minds when they saw the footage of what had happened the last time it had been attempted. High level meetings were held, which produced lower level meetings of heated debate, eventually reaching down to those of lowest rank who came up with the only sensible solution, pack up and go home.

Eventually someone came up with the bright idea of building one module inside another one, so that when the outer one failed, those in the inside module would have a chance of returning to the station.

The contraption was assembled, and a somewhat reluctant and nervous crew of two where shown how to operate the controls when it landed, the idea being to scout around the area of the cavern to see what had happened to the crystal collector, and pick up a few crystals if possible.

The double module went down, landed beautifully at the base of the upward sloping ice sheet some five hundreds metres from the cavern, and stayed there. The slope was too steep for the traction unit to get a good grip on the ice, so it moved forward a little and then slid back, ploughing the ice up and finally grinding to a halt in a pool of slush.

After several abortive attempts on the radio, which tended to hiss and crackle a lot, it was decided to travel along the ice sheet to a point where it was a little less steep, and try again. This worked quite well, and as they approached the cavern, a vicious ice storm struck. It was a total white out, and as there were no means of clearing the ice from the outer module's viewing ports, they stopped.

The ice storm only lasted a few minutes, but the wind kept blowing. Those inside couldn't see outside, but could hear the wind, and so thought the storm was still going at full blast. Those above in the Orbiter couldn't see the module, so were unable to offer any useful advice.

When their meagre rations were about to run out, the outer module began to break up, so the inner unit was called up, as the controller realised that if they didn't make it back, they would never get anyone to go down again.

The general conclusion was beginning to dawn that they weren't going to get any more crystals, either because there weren't any, or they had found them all.

This was not acceptable to the VIPs, and the pressure to acquire crystals was increased. Produce, or heads would roll.

Those who had been constipated were no longer so, whilst those who had not suffered before were joining ever lengthening queues at the medic's office to cure the newly acquired affliction.

Medical supplies were running low, and the junior medics were pressed into producing pills from anything which came to hand, just so long as they could reduce the column of applicants at the door.

Bran and Mali were enjoying life to the full. There was plenty of varied food, water, a comfortable climate, a beautiful valley to explore, and no pressure. A large lake shimmered in the diffused light of the valley, and as they approached it, thick clouds rolled in from the distant cliffs.

'Don't tell me we're going to get an ice storm here.' Bran said, looking at the dark grey clouds gathering overhead. A short while later there as a flicker of lightning high above them and the first few drops of rain fell. 'Look at that, free water falling. It's not ice, it's ordinary water. I remember, it's called rain.'

It wasn't long before they were both drenched as the rain got heavier. 'As we're so wet, we may as well get really soaked and have a swim.' Mali called out as she ran for the water's edge. With a huge splash, she hit the water and swam out towards the middle.

Bran followed, missed his footing on the bank, slipped and made a most undignified entry into the water, swallowing several gulps as he did so.

Joining Mali in the middle, he delivered a gentle reprimand for not checking the lake out first. 'What's to check?' She retorted, splashing him, 'the water's clear to the bottom, I don't think there's anything to worry about here.' The rain stopped as quickly as it had begun, and they swam around until both were out of breath. Mali set off for the shore, choosing a section of bank free of vegetation. As she was about to limb out of the water, she gasped and disappeared under the surface.

Bran swam as he had never done before, leaving a foaming wake behind him as he raced to where she had disappeared.

He dived down into a slightly cloudy area of water to see Mali entwined in a mass of writhing tentacles. Air was being forced from her lungs in a silver stream of bubbles as the creature increased its grip.

Vainly he tried to pull one of the rope-like strands from her, but it just intensified its hold. Bran panicked, he saw no way to save her. If only he had a knife he could cut her free, but there too many tentacles even if he had.

And then he remembered the crystal, it was all he had. Reaching into the pouch, he took it out and pointed it at the bulbous lump from which the tentacles sprouted. The crystal glowed and a beam of intense white light, as thin as one of the hairs of his coat lanced out. He felt rather than heard the scream as it let go of Mali and thrashed about in agony.

Grabbing one of her limp arms, he drove for the surface with all his might, lungs bursting as he broke surface.

Dragging the limp form up the bank took the last remaining strength he had, and he collapsed in a heaving heap beside her. Within seconds he had recovered enough to press down on her to force the water from her lungs, and at last she gave a deep cough and tried to sit up.

'What happened?' she managed to gasp out at last. 'It would seem something rather nasty down there took a fancy to you, and if I hadn't used the crystal, you'd still be there,' he said, between gasps for breath, 'we really should be more careful.' He added as an after thought.

They recovered slowly, still shaking a little from the shock of what might have been. 'I don't understand,' said Mali, after a while, 'I thought the tree barrier was supposed to stop anything like that from getting into the valley.' Bran was thoughtful for a moment, 'Could be that the creature evolved here by some freak of nature, although nothing else here seems harmful. Pity really, it's a great place to swim.'

'Do you think it would be wrong to get rid of the creature, I mean, it's a bit of threat really.'

'Depends how you look at it,' replied Bran, 'if we don't go in the pool, there's no threat. Anyway how could we do it? I think the crystal only works in extreme situations which we can't handle, in fact I feel certain of it.' Mali wanted her pool, and wasn't going to give up easily.

After some careful thought, she put her plan forward to him. 'If we attached something edible to a strong cord and threw it in, the creature might grab old of it, and with both of us, we could pull it out.'

'That's supposing there's only one of them.' replied Bran, not really keen on the idea. She sat there quietly for a moment. 'All right, we do it again until there's none of them left.'

Bran knew one thing for sure, if Mali set her mind to something, she would keep going at it until she won, or it was proved impossible to achieve. And he couldn't disprove it without trying it first. He may as well have agreed to it in the first place. Trouble is, she's getting more subtle, and I don't always see it coming, he thought.

They found a soft area of moss, and curled up to sleep, Mali's head resting on his flank. After their swim and having dried out, a warm scented smell drifted up from Mali's hair to Bran's nostrils, and he liked it. He suddenly felt very protective towards her, and something else, but he wasn't quite sure what.

Having slept well, they were hungry, and took their fill of berries and fruits. 'Alright, let's get it done.' said Bran, in a businesslike manner, stretching to his full height and flexing his muscles. Mali looked at him admiringly, it was almost too easy.

They went down to the lake and looked at the spot where it had happened. 'If you notice,' said Bran, 'there's no vegetation around this area, so perhaps the creature has eaten it all, no wonder it went for you like it did.' He felt it was a very profound statement of the facts as he saw them.

'So, if we look for other bare spots like this, there could be another creature there too?' Bran nodded sagely, and then realised just how big the job could be. They gathered up a small shrub, two branches with fruit on them, and a large melon-like thing, tying them together on the end of their strongest cord.

'If we run the cord around that tree first and then down to the water, it will give us a bit of leverage, and we may need it as we don't know just how big it is.' Bran was in top form with ideas, and Mali knew she had got him fired up to clear their pool of unpleasant things.

They got as close to the edge of the pool as Bran considered safe, and threw the baited cord in. It slowly sank out of sight, with a little line of bubbles rising to the surface.

Nothing else happened. 'Perhaps the crystal killed it.' offered Mali.

'Can't take a chance on that,' Bran replied, 'we'll try again.' The bait was pulled ashore and examined for signs of being nibbled at, but there were none.

The second time proved more fruitful. There was gentle pull on the line as if something was checking to see if it was alright, and then a sharp tug. 'Right, heave the sod in,' Bran yelled, 'and keep well away from it.'

It took several sharp pulls to loosen the roots, and then a mass of tentacles wrapped around their bait came into sight.

With both of them pulling with all their might, the monstrosity came into full view and slid up the bank. 'Just a bit further,' yelled Bran, 'we'll get it onto that sandy patch.' The creature was now some five metres from the water's edge, and thrashing about trying to get free as the cord had somehow got wound around it during the struggle. 'We'll tie the cord off on the tree, and leave it.'

'Will it die?' asked Mali. 'I should think so,' replied Bran, 'just the same as we would in its environment.'

They came back some time later, and the lake creature had shrivelled up to half its original size, a series of flat brown leather like strips lay around the main body, and there was no movement when Bran gave it a prod with the long bone.

'One down, and a few more to go, no doubt.' Bran exclaimed triumphantly. They untangled the cord, Bran put on some fresh bait, and they were off to look for the next bare patch on the pools edge.

'I've had an idea,' said Bran, 'if we expose the crystal to the next one, notice what the little light inside looks like, and see if it is different when the creature has died.'

Mali was impressed with his reasoning, and said so.

It took several days to clear the pool as there were five creatures in all, Bran then modified his idea with the crystal a little.

He touched the water with it, and the tiny light inside raced around a little quicker than usual. When he approached a newly hauled out creature, two lights appeared, and when the creature was dead, the crystal returned to its normal state.

After the fifth creature had been removed from the pool the crystal looked normal when he touched the water with it, and he pronounced the pool to be safe.

They were to spend many happy hours in the pool, and it became one of their favourite places to relax in.

Bran and Mali explored a large amount of the valley and found many interesting things to wonder over, but they always returned to the white domed building, as they somehow thought of it as their base.

One day Mali brought up the subject of their eventual demise, and one of them would succumb to the passing years before the other if nature was to run true to form.

As they had spent so much time together and survived so many dangerous incidents, there was a bond somewhat deeper than just companionship, although that too played its part.

The subject had come up more than once, and Bran knew deep down what Mali was basically driving at, but he felt uncertain of himself, or perhaps it was a form of shyness which held him back from taking the subject to it's ultimate conclusion. Mali was a patient creature, and gave him some considerable time to consider their prospects for the future.

One day, as Bran didn't seem to be taking the bait, Mali decided to be a little more overt, and broach the subject openly.

'When one of us has gone, so to speak, it will be awful for the other in old age, dragging one's self around, waiting to die, and no company. It doesn't have to be that way you know.'

Bran saw no way out of a frontal attack like this, and gave in. 'I suppose you mean offspring. How do you know if it would be possible for us to reproduce? We were designed to do the job of crystal collecting and survive on this planet, not procreate.'

'I hear what you're saying,' Mali replied patiently, 'but you haven't thought it out fully. Remember how you said our bodies were made from existing basic designs, and then modified physically and genetically to enable us to do the job here? Well, I think it would have involved a lot of unnecessary work to have removed the reproductive system, and adjusted the knock on effects of doing that, and as there was only supposed to be one of us here at any one time, I don't think they would have bothered.'

'I understand that,' said Bran, seeing which way the argument was going, 'but you forget the DNA was changed to suit the environment, and we were then grown to produce these bodies, so the reproductive system may not work.'

'We could give it a try,' Mali said coyly, 'after all, we have the necessary equipment to do the job, or haven't you noticed?'

Bran blushed deeply, fortunately his facial hair hid most of it, and Mali had turned her head away to spare him any more embarrassment.

'Suppose there are complications at the birth, then what do we do?' He offered as an excuse.

'If I become pregnant, it is likely the process will follow through to the end, if we give nature half a chance.' Bran could see no way out of this one, and gave up.

There was nothing for it, he would have to concede to Mali's wishes and swallow his embarrassment, which he didn't really understand in the first place.

'Well, how are we going to do it, and when?' A last desperate effort from Bran, who really knew his fate was sealed anyway.

'One, use your imagination, and two, I'll let you know when I'm ready.' Mali answered him in her best beguiling manner and a toss of her head.

Bran was relieved he had been spared the embarrassment of

immediate action, but still couldn't understand why he felt so awkward about it, for he had to admit to himself he had experienced such thoughts in the past, especially on those occasions when Mali had flaunted herself before him.

Life carried on pretty much the same as it had before, and they continued to explore their new homeland. Another long journey to the south brought them to a mountain range, although not as formidable as the last one they had to climb in order to reach their valley. It was still a barrier to what lay beyond.

Bran suspected the area on the far side were the hot lands of his dreams, and wanted to see what they were like. Mali was not too keen on the idea, as she had other things on her mind. In the end it was agreed they would explore the region, but if it was too difficult, Bran would have to make do with his dream memories.

They travelled light, only taking a supply of their strongest cords, a few bone tools and the long bone in case anything needed prodding. Food could be gathered along the way, as the valley was well stocked with fruit and berries everywhere they had been, but some would be put in the carry bags if it looked as if there could be a scarcity as they began their climb.

Their only problem was the transportation of water. Mali had found two large gourds which she had hollowed out, and these were taken, to be filled when they thought they had reached their last water supply.

As they neared the foothills, vegetation began to thin out, so supplies were put into the carry bags, and a hearty meal taken. Small streams ran down from the rocks above which supplied their drinking water, although it often had a strange metallic taste.

As they climbed higher it was apparent that the hot zone on the other side of the range was devoid of cloud cover, as a clear dark blue, almost purple sky was seen. The cloud layer began just north of the range, over their valley.

The light that the temperate and cold zones of the planet received was due to transmission through the cloud layer, the light of the naked sun being far to high for life to have developed within it's burning glare, The cold zone was devoid of sunlight anyway, as it was on the far side of the planet and in perpetual darkness.

During their stay in the valley, they had noticed the hair of their coats was a little thinner and finer in texture, due to the difference in ambient temperature of their new home compared to that of the ice fields where they had begun their lives. A much better diet, and being more balanced, also helped in their attaining a greatly improved physical state.

Soon there was no sign of vegetation as the ground grew more stony, and the streams had dwindle to a trickle, while the occasional hiss of a steam vent was the only sound apart from their foot falls, and the odd dislodged stone. As they neared what they thought was the top of the range they were confronted by a sheer wall of vertical rock towering above them, and far too steep to climb. 'Looks like a dead end.' said Bran, disappointment clearly sounding in his voice.

'Look, there's a small cleft in the rock over there,' Mali pointed out, 'we could go a little further if you really want to.' It was just wide enough for them to enter, but in single file with Bran leading the way.

It twisted and turned, still climbing, and the temperature was rising. Mali was about to call a halt to the venture, when Bran exclaimed excitedly 'There's something different up ahead.'

On a bend in the cleft ahead the walls glowed red, and Bran stopped dead in his tracks. 'If those rocks are red hot, and they look like it, why don't I feel the heat?' Slowly he edged forward, ready to back up quickly if it got too hot, but it didn't. As he rounded the bend, he let out a yell, 'Mali, you should see this!'

'I can't' she answered, 'you're in the way.'

'All right, I'll back up a bit, hunker down, and you'll have to climb over the top of me.' She gasped when she saw the inferno before her. Far below, the whole area seemed to glow deep red, with wisps of smoke arising from holes in the ground, while rocky pinnacles shimmered in the blazing heat.

A pool of something molten heaved and bubbled with a bizarre life of its own, and small jets of liquid occasionally spurting upwards, to later fall back with a lurid splash.

As she watched, a tall pinnacle of rock, destabilized by the soft ground beneath it, toppled over sending a vivid yellow splash of liquid rock skywards.

Mali backed away from the glare, bumping into Bran as she did so, and they both shuffled back down the cleft to a cooler area. 'How can it be so hot?' Mali enquired, 'and yet our valley which is not so far away is cool?'

'It's the mountains which protect us,' said Bran, 'and the cloud layer, without them we'd cook as well. I can remember a lot of strange places, but nothing quite like this.'

The stifling dry dusty air from the hot lands blew up through the rift every now and again, making their throats sore with its sulphurous fumes. 'May as well go back down,' said Bran, 'there's nothing for us here, but we at least know what's on the other side of the mountains.'

They had to go up on their hind legs in order to turn around, as the rift at this point was so narrow.

Half way down, Mali spotted an opening in the rock wall which they had missed on their upwards trek, as it was angled away from the main track.

'Wonder what's in there.' she said, wanting to appear a little more adventurous than she really was. The hole was big enough for them to enter easily, and began a gentle downwards slope. The rocks seemed to emit their own light, although it was very feeble compared to the tunnels back in their ice world.

Twenty metres in the passage ended in a large cavern, and they stopped just in time. The pathway also ended, in a drop of some five metres to a pool of black looking water. As their eyes grew accustomed to the gloom they could see a little more detail. The walls were hung with long ribbons of some grey coloured growth, and hanging down from some of the thicker strands were bunches of huge translucent grapes. As they watched, one fell off making a small splash.

A faint ripple some few metres away grew into a small tidal wave as something very hungry hurried to grab it. A snake like head broke from the waters, opened cavernous jaws and swallowed the grape as if it had been a pea.

The head slowly turned to face them, two large malevolent eyes stared at them for a moment, and then it ducked down into the water out of sight. A faint ripple on the surface came towards them and they fled back up the tunnel, and out into the open air.

'That was rather unpleasant.' said Bran, trying to make light of what could have been a disaster.

They carried on down the rift, and felt relieved when the first plants began to appear. They were a bit straggly, very thin, and dull in colour due to the arduous conditions in which they tried to live. They eagerly awaited the first stream of clear water to appear, as the gourds had long been emptied.

At last the rift opened out to the rolling gravel beds which lay all along the bottom edge of the mountain chain, and in the distance they could see the familiar trees and bushes of the valley.

'Well, we're back home again, and in one piece', said Mali, as they trotted out onto the soft green grass of the lower plains, 'can't wait to have a swim and get clean again.'

The first sizeable pool was soon made cloudy with the dust they had collected on their trip up the mountain, and then they lay side by side at the pool's edge, to dry out their coats in the warm scented air.

Far above them, the space station continued to reel around the planet, the crew finding all sorts of interesting things to do to spin out the time before the station was shut down, along with the most lucrative job any of them had ever had.

They had long ago given up any hope of actually finding any crystals, as all the pictures sent back from the robot explorers showed no sign of them, only the holes where they had lain.

When things were going well, someone always had to spoil it. A bright little spark, who was an aid to the assistant who helped the second in command of the data retrieval system, had thumbed through the pictures sent back from the search robots, and found a stunning graphic of a very large lump of the red crystal bearing rock. It was huge.

The information was passed back up the line to the chief engineer in charge of crystal gathering, who should have known better and used his basic instincts. He thrust aside his better judgment, and casting all cares to the proverbial winds, called a meeting of the senior staff and showed them the picture.

The general opinion of the meeting declared that there was a good chance the block of red rock, because of it's size, may well hold some crystals, and a great deal of kudos would be obtained for the station if they could retrieve them. As the co-ordinates of the rock were obtainable from the picture, a special probe was sent down with measuring equipment on board to ascertain its actual size. It was massive, an estimate of several tonnes was bandied about, but no one was quite sure.

A massive carrier was constructed with a single door hinged at the top, complete with seals, and remote controlled hydraulic grappling arms to pull the rock into the box-like vessel.

The size of the vessel was based on the largest loading bay they had, and it would be touch and go as to whether the rock would fit into the carrier.

The great day came at last, and the carrier was sent down to land only a few metres away form the huge block of red stone. This was seen as a very good omen indeed. The huge door opened upwards on its hydraulic rams and the whole unit crept forward on its traction unit until it was almost touching the block of rock. The grappling arms extended to reach around to the furthest side of the rock, closed, and began retracting to pull the colossal red stone into the carrier. Having got the stone inside, the huge doors swung down on their hinges, locked, sealed, and the whole thing was ready for the journey back up to the space station.

Four:
Freedom

ALL WENT WELL with the lift up into orbit. The carrier was manoeuvred into position outside the loading bay doors, and the clamps locked it securely in place. The air was pumped out of the bay, the huge doors opened, and the carrier was drawn in. The doors closed, sealed, and the bay was refilled with air.

One of the brighter engineers realised the atmosphere inside the carrier would be toxic to them, so a large flexible pipe was connected to the carrier, and the corrosive atmosphere was vented to space. The carrier was filled with air and emptied several times to flush out any remaining noxious gases, and then the doors were opened to see what their prize block of stone had to offer.

It was unfortunate for those on board the station that their atmosphere differed so much from that of the planet. As the station's air was bled into the carrier, the rock reacted with it, converting to a thin red mud like liquid which bubbled and frothed vigorously. As the doors opened, the red tide flowed out, sweeping several members of the team off their feet and swirling around the legs of those a little further back.

The crew who were able to, jumped or climbed onto anything in sight which offered some sort of sanctuary from the liquid, and saved them for a while. Air rushed into the carrier to replace the liquid rock which had flowed out, and so more of it converted to join that which had spewed out before.

Those at the very back of the loading bay raced for the exit door, but as it was only a small one, several were flattened in the process, and the door was slammed shut.

In the main control room, where the whole event was being monitored on the viewing screens, they were paralysed with shock at the speed of what had happened, and the decimation of the loading bay crew.

Pressure in the loading bay rose as the stone underwent further changes, and gasses were released, forcing the red liquid into the wiring conduits and the air conditioning trunking, whence it proceeded to permeate the internal workings of the station, seeping into every nook and cranny.

The general stampede to reach the upper docking bay and escape the horrors below was something to behold. Fortunately for those who made it, a large bulk freighter had docked, and there was a mad rush to throw out the remaining goods and then scramble aboard.

The elderly captain of the vessel was ordered to blast off at once, but as this wasn't according to his schedule, a heated argument broke out, the captain was overcome with confusion and someone gave the order on his behalf, doing a very good imitation of his quite distinctive voice.

Everyone heaved a sigh of relief as the ship closed its hatches, released the holding clamps and accelerated away from the stricken space station. Unfortunately, one of the crew had a tiny speck of something nasty on his shoe, the red liquid rock

In their innocence, everyone on board the freighter relaxed and the station's members who had escaped, recounted the story, which was taken with the proverbial pinch of salt by those who manned the freighter.

The tiny speck of sludge had got scraped off on one of the rungs of the ladder leading to the upper decks. It hung there for a moment, and then fell to the deck below, slipping through a gap in the floor plates and down to the below decks area. Here it found plenty of material to metabolise and increased in volume at an amazing rate. Soon the lower decks were awash with the foaming red tide as it converted anything it touched. The old freighter thundered on through star lit space, heading for its home planet.

It had gone about one tenth of the way by the time the whole of the lower decks had been flooded, and it was now creeping up the ducting into the main cargo bay. Here it found plenty to ingest, and multiplied accordingly.

One of the freighter's crew, doing a routine service job, tried to open the hatch to the next level down, but it was jammed. This was not an uncommon occurrence, so he got a hydraulic jack, put it place and turned on the power.

The hatch resisted, so he turned up the power, the hatch buckled under the immense pressure and then opened, and in came the red sludge. He was knocked off is feet and submerged before he could raise the alarm, so the sludge slowly and quietly worked its way up through the ship.

Back on the space station, the red sludge had also been hard at work, foaming into every tiny space until it ran out of oxygen, and then it reverted back into its original form of solid rock, and not one purple crystal in sight.

The occasional rain shower swept down through the valley on soft and gentle breezes, keeping everything green and lush, and filling the little streams which meandered between the gently sloping hills and their clumps of trees and fruit bushes.

A few insects had been found by sitting very still and looking for movement, which was the only time they were noticeable. Most had such good camouflage and were so slow moving that they were passed by unnoticed most of the time.

One thing missing from the streams were fish, and Bran thought that they were one evolutionary line which hadn't developed for some reason, although a few crustaceans had been found clinging to the underside of submerged stones.

As Bran wasn't keen on fishing, and they didn't seem to need animal protein, he didn't miss their presence.

They were returning to the white dome from another exploration of their valley, Mali jogging along in front, when Bran found he was admiring the shape of her hind quarters and legs. He felt his heart begin to beat a little bit faster, and a faint dizzy feeling seemed to hover just behind his eyes.

Mali stopped, turned around with a smile on her face, and that wicked look she reserved for special teasing occasions.

Bran suddenly felt very hot and bothered, and his heart began to pound. Without thinking, he walked on until he was almost touching her, and as she was in oestrus, the gentle breeze wafted the pheromone she was emitting straight into his nostrils. The sensors in his nose picked them up, a surge of adrenaline coursed through his veins, several glands went into over drive and his vision blurred.

Mali gave her rear end a little twitch, raised her tail slightly, and then swung it to one side. Before he knew what he had done, Bran mounted her as gently as his hormones would allow, and then nature took over with a degree of enthusiasm only nature can produce.

Afterwards they lay side by side on the grassy bank by a stream, still trembling a little.

'There, it wasn't all that bad, was it?' Mali did enjoy teasing him.

Bran gave her a generous slap across her rump saying, 'You are an unmitigated hussy, madam.' and promptly fell asleep.

Some time later as Mali's middle began to thicken, Bran thought they ought to find some way of making paper or something similar, so that their not inconsiderable amount of knowledge would not be forgotten, and could be passed on to future generations. Various plants were tried, but nothing had the fibrous texture necessary.

It was while they were exploring a new region of their world that the problem was solved.

A long line of water plants fringed a large lake, and at the top of their willowy stems large tuffs of fine white hairs swayed in the light breeze.

After much trial and error, Mali managed to spin some very fine threads to make the necessary sieve to trap the pulp in, while Bran found if the fluffy reed heads were pounded in water, they formed a fine slurry from which they could make a crude paper. A pen, and ink for writing was easily extracted from a hard gall like growth found on some bushes. The whole thing would need refining, but that would come in time, and they had plenty of that.

They still considered the white dome as the focal point of their valley, always returning to it after an exploration, but rarely going inside except to marvel at its pristine whiteness and symmetry.

On one occasion, when they were standing next to the dome, Mali asked if Bran's crystal still had it's pinpoint of light within. 'Don't know, it's been ages since we used it,' Bran replied, 'don't see why not.' He took the little crystal from its pouch and passed it to Mali. 'Yes, it's still there,' she said, 'but I can only just see it.' She paused, looking perplexed, 'Wait a minute, there are two lights now.' Suddenly the crystal seemed to glow, and Mali's eyes went out of focus.

Slowly she turned and began to walk towards the entrance, Bran tied to follow, but was rooted to the spot, his legs wouldn't work. A flash of panic ran through him as Mali reached the centre of the dome, and slowly extended her arm up as high as it would go. The crystal was now blazing with light, and as she let it go, it drifted up to the top of the dome, and vanished from sight.

A blinding flash of light was accompanied by a shock wave which seemed to shake the whole valley. When their eyes returned to normal and they could see again, the crystal had grown in size many times over, and now protruded from the top of the dome, while a small point of it poked through to the inside.

Mali joined Bran outside, and they both stood there, staring at the huge crystal as it seemed to suck the very light out of the sky, and the dome glowed as it had never done before. 'What the hell was that all about?' asked Bran.

Mali had that faraway look in her eyes, as if she knew something he didn't. Very softly she said, 'Now it's complete.' Slowly the glowing dome returned to its normal state and the crystal was just a crystal. A connection had been made which would have far reaching effects in the future, but they were not to know that, as yet.

Life carried on as it had before, but Mali was getting close to term, and Bran worried about the consequences of giving birth without the conventional help.

They had been resting on a grassy bank beside a large pool when Bran decided to got for a swim. He plunged into the water with a mighty splash, drenching Mali, and disappeared from sight. After a while, with no sign of him, Mali began to panic. At that moment, Bran reappeared looking very excited. 'Hey, you should see this,' he called, treading water, 'there's a whole cave system down here. I could see a faint light under the bank and went to have look. There's a cave which leads into several others, and there's air down there, you can breathe.' He explained how the caves were lit by something similar to the glowing moss back in their ice world caves and tunnels. Mali wanted to go down and have a look, but Bran thought it too risky as she was so far advanced in her pregnancy.

The planet changed orbit to its other sun again, and during the rotational flip over there were storms for a while, with lashing rain and high winds.

When they wanted to dry out, they sort shelter in the white dome, and were amazed to find it only took a few minutes for their coats to become dry and fluffy again.

Shortly after the weather had stabilised, Mali's time came, and she tended to hover around the dome rather than go far afield as they usually did each day, but Bran didn't understand why and queried it.

'Look,' said Mali, 'my teats have waxed up, and that's a sure sign that I'll give birth soon.' Bran now followed her around like a small puppy, never more than a stones throw away.

They had just woken up and taken a light meal, when Mali, with a frightened look in her eyes, gave a little squeal. 'Ok, what can I do?' asked Bran, putting an arm around her shoulder. 'Nothing really, we'll just have to let nature take her course, I'm sure everything will be alright.' Bran was not convinced.

After two more cries of pain, Mali went into the dome and Bran tried to follow, but he couldn't set foot inside the entrance as is legs refused to move.

Now he was really frightened, 'I can't get in.' he called out in anguish.

'I don't think you're meant to,' Mali replied between little whimpers, 'the dome will take care of everything.' Bran retired to a soft patch of grass just outside the dome, and lay down. He felt utterly useless now, as it was he who usually took all the risks, did the defending where necessary, and made the decisions, or so he thought.

The crystal on top of the dome was now glowing brightly, and a soft hum filled the air. The dome was now linked to something far, far away, and energies flowed between them.

A series of deep grunts, each followed by the sharp hiss of expelled air, emanated from the dome. Bran leapt to his feet and had only taken three steps when there was a blinding flash of light, and for a moment the whole valley seemed to shimmer. This was followed by a sharp cry of pain, a low moan, and then complete silence.

The light in the crystal dimmed, winked once and went out, the energies which had ebbed and flowed around the dome were gone, and he stood there in the stillness of the valley, wondering if his world had finally fallen to pieces.

With his heart in his mouth and trembling slightly, Bran went into the dome expecting the worst, and saw Mali had struggled to her feet, and a tiny foal was feeding greedily from her swollen teats.

She smiled at him and said, 'They say the first is the worst, so it can only get better.'

'We're not going through that again Mali, no way.' he replied, trying to sound firm and commanding, but failing miserably.

'Oh yes we are, we're going to build up a herd.' This was not the time to argue, so Bran let it drop for the time being. Later, Mali brought the little foal out into the open after its initial feed, and introduced it to Bran with much sniffing and blowing of breath.

It was still a little wobbly on its feet, and damp, but the warm breeze wafting up the valley soon dried its coat out so that it looked like a fluffy ball of wool on legs.

Bran was beginning to feel emotions he had no idea he was capable of, and it surprised him not a little.

It wasn't long before the threesome were trotting along the soft grassy tracks of the valley, the foal having quickly learnt to co-ordinate it's leg movements to let it safely gambol about on it's own.

'In case you hadn't noticed, we have a little girl,' Mali said cheerfully, 'I wonder what the next one will be?'

Bran didn't say anything, he'd handle that situation when the time came, at least, that's what he intended.

On her rich milk the foal grew at an enormous rate, and a name was sought for her. Col was decided on as it somehow suited her bright and bouncy nature.

It wasn't long before she was weaned, and Mali began her coy little suggestion to Bran again. He wasn't having any of it, but nature being what it is things got a little out of his control, and Mali was very skilled at turning his hormones on full tilt, and there was little he could do about that.

As Mali's middle began to thicken again, Bran asked her why she felt she had to go into the dome to give birth.

She thought for a while before she spoke, wondering how to explain the inexplicable.

'I just somehow knew it was right,' she said at last, 'remember what we are, separate beings in bodies. What we went through just to be here should have convinced you of that. Where was the new being or spirit going to come from? There were only the two of us here, so it had to come from somewhere else, and I think the dome somehow arranged that.'

It was at this point that Bran finally realised that they were part of a plan, a readjustment of nature, call it what you will, and it was totally outside their control.

The second, third, and fourth births were progressively easier for Mali, and by the time the fifth birth came along, Col, the first born, had already taken on some of her mothers coquettish mannerisms, and added a few of her own. She could often be seen with Kos, the second born, in attendance, a handsome young male, complete with a bemused look of adoration in his eyes.

Bran and Mali were both aware of the dangers of interbreeding, but could see no solution to the problem. The only conclusion they could come to was that the dome would somehow sort it out.

'You don't need a mirror, just look at Col,' Bran said, giving Mali a dig in the ribs. She turned, and smiling sweetly said, 'I haven't heard you complaining lately.' And with that she gave him a cuff around the head with her tail as she trotted past him down the path.

Just look at those hips swinging, Bran thought to himself as his hormones took over once again, and he followed his beloved Mali down the track to a place of her choosing.

The fifth generation produced the first of the mutants, in so far that they were born with only one pair of legs, the trunk foreshortened and a little more stocky in build.

Somehow it came as no surprise to Bran and Mali, as the dome began to cause a reversion back to the normal human form. They were able to stand upright in the normal humanoid stance, and although so different, were accepted by all as a natural progression towards what the dome eventually had in mind.

Subsequent generations became even more humanoid, losing the beautiful thick white coat of their predecessors as it was no longer needed.

Bran and Mali at last succumbed to old age, although their lives had been extended considerably by the forces at work in the valley. It was a sad day for the little nation when they both passed away, locked in each others arms and looking quite contented with what they had achieved.

✳ ✳ ✳

One day, someone noticed the crystal on top of the dome was missing, and the structure no longer had that mysterious glow when entered for the birthing process.

They concluded that the forces which had fashioned their race now considered their work was done, and had withdrawn.

The caves found under the pool bank so long ago had been explored, and many interesting things found, not the least of which were small nuggets of a metal which could be melted, and that brought about a whole new science of metallurgy.

Gradually the stone lands between the temperate and cold zones were put to good use, and even some of the ice world of Bran and Mali surrendered up some of their mysteries to the ever probing race from the warm zone.

Once the green valley had been populated to a point where it could sustain no more, the elected council decreed a control of the birth rate, which was agreed to by all.

They erected a massive statue of Bran and Mali from the rare metal found in the caves. Every hair faithfully and lovingly carved, and beneath it was a plaque inscribed with the words:

'IN REMEMBRANCE AND GRATITUDE,
LEST WE FORGET FROM WHENCE WE CAME'

The End